The Game Changer

The Game Changer

Tina Samo

The Game Changer

Published by
Lighthouse Christian Publishing
SAN 257-4330
5531 Dufferin Drive
Savage, Minnesota, 55378
United States of America

www.lighthousechristianpublishing.com

Chapter 1

"Watch out!"

The screen door snapped back into place, barely missing the awkwardly stacked boxes as I backed into the room.

I turned to see Zeek's grin. "That was close."

I handed the box off and headed out to the truck for the next load. As I dragged another box to the tailgate, ready to lug it in with the others, I glanced up. In the distance I noticed the old corn bin and chuckled to myself again.

A year ago, I would have thought this whole situation was just a crazy coincidence. But I knew better now. The fact that Zeek and his mother were moving into *this* exact house was another you-can't-possibly-believe-this-was-an-accident deal. I was getting better at recognizing God at work.

It was like looking at those 3-D pictures: at first all I could see was the background design, but as I kept looking, the picture would eventually pop out. Once I got the hang of how to see the hidden pictures, they would practically jump out at me. I hefted the box to my shoulder and thought back to when the picture wasn't so clear.

Brazon had issued the challenge. And we all knew that Zeek loved a challenge. He couldn't turn one down. That was his problem. That, and the fact that he tried too hard to fit in. He'd do anything we told him to, just so long as we let him hang around us.

He flipped his greasy bangs back with a I'm-ready-to-do-this-thing look and grabbed the lowest rung. As I watched him scale the narrow ladder attached to the side of the looming corn bin, I wondered at the half-witted smile tugging at his face. What was he thinking? He paused for a moment, slowly sizing up his remaining climb, then with a burst of energy, surged upward with an unusual eagerness. I could see his silhouette as it became smaller and smaller, finally swallowed in the darkness.

How many times would he fall for these stupid pranks? There he was, certainly at the top of the bin by now, probably proud of himself for accepting such a dare and performing so well. An unwelcomed picture flashed in my mind: the last time we publically humiliated Zeek in front of the entire fifth and sixth grade PE class. Our plan had been just as simple. First, taunt the opposing team into throwing all of their dodge balls. Then, convince Zeek to be our front man and lead the attack. When he was poised and ready to throw the first missile, we would sneak up and jerk his gym shorts to the floor. The stunt was sure to earn us detention, but the laughs would be worth it.

What I didn't count on was the guilt. It began even as Brazon was going over the plan in the locker room. By the time we actually grabbed the hem of Zeek's shorts; my gut was burning, especially when I caught the hurt look in Zeek's eyes as the laughter roared in my ears.

"I made it! Hey - it's great up here! Anybody else coming up?" I was jerked back to the present.

"Naaa, not tonight," shouted Brazon into the darkness.

"Ahh, well, I guess I'll come on down then," Zeek yelled back, trying to sound nonchalant.

Little did he know that Brazon, Triton, and I had other plans for him.

I thought back to the remorse I felt after that last school incident. The detention and call home did nothing to tame my guilt. Only after talking with my youth pastor and praying for forgiveness did I feel relief.

"C'mon. Now!" Triton ordered in a half-whisper.

How had I let myself fall into the old routine again? I remembered asking God for strength to walk away from the next scheme, because I *knew* there would be another. And this was it. And I was caught up in it again.

Reluctantly I followed as my two best friends raced to the shed where we had been earlier that afternoon. The deserted old farmhouse watched as we quietly slid the broken shed door back and retrieved our three stashed guns. We raced back just in time to make out Zeek's scrawny shape as he made his way back down the ladder.

"Ah-ah-ah. Not so fast!" Triton challenged in a menacing tone. "You're not in a big hurry to leave, are you?"

"I guess . . . guess not . . . why? Are you coming up?" he asked in a voice that told us he knew better.

"Us? Naw. But we figured you might like to spend some extra time up there, seeing as how it's so great and all," Brazon taunted.

"Uhh . . . well, I would . . . but listen, I told my dad I'd be home by 9:30. It's gotta be that late by now."

"Oh, I don't think so," sneered Brazon. He turned to me, "What do you think, Razz?"

"I don't think so," I joined in half-heartedly.

"Really guys, I gotta go."

"Really guys," mocked Triton as he lifted his gun to his shoulder. *"Really. I gotta go."* The snap of his cocking gun echoed in the stillness of the night.

"What's that? What . . . what do you guys got?" Zeek's trembling voice betrayed his fear.

"Who? Us? Nothing. We got nothing at all!" lied Brazon with a knowing grin.

But as Zeek lowered his foot to the next rung, a blast shattered the night and a PING resounded as the BB hit the side of the bin.

"Geez! What the . . . " Zeek sounded shaken.

"Well Zeeky, buddy, you said you were enjoying it up there, so we thought you could provide a little entertainment because we're kinda bored down here. We've never seen anybody do a dance on a corn bin." SNAP! Triton cocked his BB gun. "So, you see, we'd like you to head right back up to the top there and give us a little show." The silence was stunned again by the crack of Triton's gun.

"Come on, guys." Zeek's voice was uneven and shaky.

"Take your best aim, Razz. He just doesn't seem to be convinced yet."

I wiped my sweaty palms and thought again about this afternoon's secret session. Brazon had taken the lead, as usual. After he outlined the plan, I voiced my objections. We would be trespassing on private property. Someone could get hurt. But Brazon and Triton only scoffed at my worries. I was fairly proud of myself for not backing down during their barrage of name-calling. But I fell for Triton's logical reasoning: "Listen, Razz. Do you think we'd ever *really* hurt Zeek? Naw. This is just fun. He doesn't have to try it if he doesn't want."

I half-heartedly cocked my gun and pointed at Zeek's foot.

"Come on, what are you waiting for?" Brazon sounded disgusted.

"Yea - he's on his way down again!" Triton added with urgency in his voice.

Well, we had agreed to keep him on the bin just until he gave us a good laugh. Maybe after each of us had one shot - just one shot. As I pressured the trigger, I purposely swing the nose of my gun into the darkness. CRACK!

"Man! You shoot like my grandma!" Triton watched me in disbelief.

"Umm?" a faint voice called, "I'm coming down now, okay?"

"No way! We ain't seen our show yet." Brazon was obviously enjoying this. He took on the ringmaster's tone, "Introducing 'Zeek the Freak' doing a dangerous balancing act. Step back folks, in case he falls."

"C'mon, guys . . ."

"Let's try again, 'huh?" BOOM! Another reminder that the game was not over.

"Okay. okay." Zeek's voice cracked. "Please?"

"Okay," I quickly approved. "You can come on down now," I added in a commanding voice.

"What? Are you kidding?" Brazon demanded. "We're just starting to have fun."

"It's getting old to me," I said, trying to sound bored. "Let's go find some *real* fun."

"I'm having a good enough time here, how about you, Triton?"

"Yea, I need to practice my shot a little more." SNAP. "We haven't even gotten close." BANG - PING! The BB rebounded off of the ladder, causing Zeek to jump up a rung. "That's more like it. Faster! Now! C'mon guys!"

Triton and Brazon simultaneously raised their guns and took aim. Shots rang out again. Out of the corner of his eye, Brazon caught me standing motionless.

"What the?"

"This is stupid. I'm going."

"Awww, look who's wimping out," mocked Brazon.

"I'm not wimping out. I'm just bored."

"Oh? You're just bored?" mimicked Triton. "I think you're just a little mama's boy."

"I am not!" I defended myself.

"Really? Well if that's the case, let's have a little more fun, then we'll all take off. How does that sound to you, Freaky Zeeky?"

"Uhh," I could hear Zeek sniff. I felt a sudden twist in my stomach. "Hey guys . . ." he pleaded, "I really gotta go. My . . . my . . . dad's gonna kill me."

"Or what's left of you?" taunted Brazon while cocking his gun. He and Triton opened up on Zeek and after what seemed hours of blasting and cracking, a deadening silence fell. Brazon raised his eyebrows at us and angled his head. In the darkness, I could hear muffled sounds coming from far up on the bin. It sounded like crying. Zeek was at the top of the bin, trying now to quiet himself. My arms and legs began to ache and my stomach knotted and churned. A voice inside of my head kept saying, *"This is wrong and you know it. Get out of here."* But I knew I should stay, if only to help Zeek.

"You gotta be kidding," Brazon laughed to himself. "He's actually crying - what a baby!"

Triton rolled his eyes. "Unreal. What does he think we're gonna do, kill him?"

"Yea, really. This is lame," I added in a disinterested voice, trying once again to end the game.

"Hey! Razz isn't laughing!" Triton called up into the darkness. "Come on Zeek, make us laugh!" Silence.

Then in a malicious voice, Brazon added, "We're waiting."

"B-but . . . how?" A sniff betrayed Zeek's casual tone.

"Oh," Brazon taunted, "I don't know. What'd make ya laugh, Razz?"

Seeing another chance, I replied, "Nothing here. I'm out." I let my arm drop and drug my gun as I headed to my bike.

"You just don't know how to have a good time," shouted Brazon to my back.

Ignoring his jab, I kept walking.

"I think we have two babies with us, Brazon. What do you think?"

"I think I ain't getting paid to babysit."

I kept walking.

"Who's the bigger baby, do you suppose?" Triton kept it up.

"They must be twins, I guess, That's why they're such good buddies."

I slowed momentarily. I knew what they were trying to do, and it was working. I felt sorry for Zeek, but none of us would actually want to be considered Zeek's friend. That's the way it had been ever since he moved to our town five years ago. We couldn't find a more willing stooge. We could count on him to fall for every one of our tricks. Anyone else would've gotten mad, gotten even, or gotten away from us; but Zeek seemed to thrive on the attention. At least, that's what I told myself. After all, we were the only ones that would let him near us. He never seemed to mind.

Until tonight. This was different. We weren't just making fun of the way he walked, or giving him a dunk as he tried to drink from the water fountain at school, or hiding all of his clothes after gym class so he had to ask the PE teacher for help in his underwear. No, tonight was different. And I didn't like it.

Zeek was truly scared. The way we were treating him was wrong. No, I wouldn't let their name-calling get the best of me. They knew Zeek and I weren't actually buddies, and for the first time that night I found myself not caring so much what they thought.

I turned around and looked at them as I reached my bike. "Yea, right. Whatever."

As I rode away, I could hear their sarcastic calls. "Whatsa matter, Razz? Your daddy gonna be real mad at you too?"

"Don't count on us for any more fun."

"... yea, what a loser ..."

But worse than anything they could have said was the banging and cracking of their guns against the stillness of the night.

I briefly replayed the scene in my mind and fit in possible endings where I stood up to Brazon and Triton. But the picture always became clouded by the thought of me taking Zeek's place - becoming their stooge, their scapegoat, their outcast. I couldn't handle that thought, so I rode on in the warm summer night.

On my way home, I had to pass the corner that led to Zeek's house. As I neared the street, I could faintly make out a dim light seeping through the torn, threadbare curtains that were always drawn. I slowed and swerved onto the sidewalk that ran in front of the house. Something drew me to that one front window, and I found myself moving so slowly that I had to concentrate to keep my balance. I could see the outline of a slumped figure as it passed in front of the shaded, open window. A loud belch and the crunching of a can echoed down the empty street.

I had been by this house many times when I was just riding around looking for something to do. It was the lone, corner house on a half-empty street leading out of town. Across from it was the old garage that used to house the volunteer fire department, but it had been deserted for years. On the other side of the house was the worn barn that the school rented to park the buses during the year.

One of our biggest kicks during the year was when the custodians parked the buses outside so that they could be washed out. We'd sneak into each bus and dig between seats for money, gum, candy, or maybe a juicy love-letter. And, of course, Zeek had to stand guard for us and keep tabs on which bus was being cleaned. We came close to getting caught once, but Zeek took the rap instead. Our burly bus driver grabbed him by the collar of his coat and asked what he was doing. He took the whole thing like a real pro and never once leaked that we were in on it too.

I quietly stepped down from my bike and slid soundlessly behind the half-dead oak tree that was a silent witness to all that happened in the Zeekman house. It knew the true story of why Zeek's mom up and left without a word to anyone, not the half-witted excuse that Zeek gave everyone about her visiting a sick aunt. We had sure dished out our own suggestions about why she left. I cringed as I remembered the sarcastic insinuations we had thrown at him through the years. But that half-rotted tree knew the truth. And it knew about Old Man Zeekman's temper. But then, we all knew about that.

I hesitated for just a moment, wondering why I was even there. I knew it was crazy, but I felt myself drawn to watch what would unfold. I positioned myself carefully behind that old oak and became the witness to a scene that seemed straight out of a movie.

The first part of the show was a one-man act. Old Man Zeekman was the star. The worn, thin curtain through which I viewed the scene created an eerie atmosphere as the actor took the stage. After tossing his empty beer can with a rumbling burp, he passed back by the kitchen window on his way to get another. I heard the door slam shut with a string of obscenities.

"Wha--? Ten to ten?" Belch. Swearing. "Idiot kid. He'll be learnin' a lesson or two 'bout lying to his ole man." There was a threat to his voice that made me shudder. He turned and I could see his outline as he hunched over, laboring intently with something. Swearing accentuated his frustration as he struggled awkwardly to slide his belt through the loops. I could imagine his pants shifting down an inch or two under the weight of his massive barrel chest and pregnant-looking beer belly. Even worse, I could picture the damage he could do with that belt.

As he stumbled from room to room, kicking everything that neared his path and muttering every obscenity I'd ever heard, I suddenly felt uncomfortable with the idea of being a hidden observer. In the darkness, I caught a glimpse of my bike that now lay deserted on the sidewalk. The thought of sneaking back to it and away from this place became more appealing as I heard a loud crash escape from one of the back rooms. I tried convincing myself that Zeek would just get punished for being late, then would be sent to bed grounded.

I was ready to make a move to my bike when I heard a faint clicking sound. Panic screamed that Old Man Zeekman was sneaking up behind me. I stood frozen, my heartbeat pounding in my ears. A loud THUD came from inside the house, followed by a burst of anger. My breath escaped in a heavy whoosh as I realized Zeek's dad was still inside.

Then what was the sound? The clicking continued, but now faster and louder, as if it were getting closer and closer. There was something familiar about that sound, but I couldn't pinpoint its source. As my mind raced around in circles, a figure burst out of the darkness. Zeek dropped his rickety bike and raced towards the back of the house.

I watched the second scene even more intensely than the first. Old Man Zeekman was in the kitchen again, sitting at the table now, smoking a cigarette. I could only catch the outline of his stubbled head and his hand methodically moving to his mouth. At the same time, I watched Zeek try to slip in the side door and make his way silently to safety. I held my breath as he expertly opened the screen door without a sound, padded inside, then noiselessly eased the door slowly back into place. I lost sight of him, but strained to hear him move inside. Nothing. I could only imagine him sneaking cautiously toward his bedroom. I mentally cheered him on.

The weight of the silence was so suffocating that as I let out an uneven breath of air, I was certain that it could be heard for miles. I inadvertently gasped as the silhouette of Old Man Zeekman suddenly sprang to its feet and the crashing force of a fist pounded the table.

"Where is he?" came with a heavy thud.

Zeek must have panicked. I could hear with sharp clarity his sudden steps as he raced to his bedroom. Then a door slammed shut and the click of a lock.

He made it! I breathed the same sigh of relief that every audience member does after a scary part of the movie, just when it seems the main character is safe. But then the slow, eerie background music plays and everyone knows something awful is going to happen. There was no background music that night. There didn't need to be.

I saw him turn and lumber from the room swinging the belt as he went. His thick arms hung awkwardly away from his body. My mind flashed back to when Zeek told us that his dad finally got a job at the factory. He did manual labor. We all laughed. All that meant was the factory had a new goon. That's what they called the guy dumb enough to carry those heavy bags that wouldn't fit on the fork lift. Suddenly it didn't seem so funny.

I could hear him taking the stairs two or three at a time. He didn't say a word. He pounded on the door a few times, then it sounded like he broke it down. I couldn't see anything through the dark window upstairs. I didn't have to. I could hear . . . too much. Zeek's cries of fear like a whimpering dog. The slapping and cracking of a belt without a conscience. Painful crying and pleading to stop. Half-sentences and curses uttered from a man too enraged to speak. A thud from a fist that found its mark. Groans and screams. A scuff and a sickening thump from a boot that finished the job. An unintentional cry, then gasping coughs. Then silence.

The instinct to run overpowered any of my remaining morbid curiosities. I darted from my safe hiding place and onto my bike in one swift motion, pumping my way back home as if for my life. Muffled shouts haunted my ride as I made my escape.

"Always tryin' ta get away with sumpthin." Thud. "Maybe this'll learn ya . . ." Crack. " . . . ain't made of money . . . do your part . . . "

As I rounded the street corner, I could see the lights from my own house a block away. All I wanted now was to sneak in and forget. Suddenly I noticed a chill in the air. As I reached up to pull my jersey tighter around my neck, I was surprised to find it drenched with sweat. I ran the back of my hand across my clammy forehead. My lower jaw began to shake uncontrollably, and I knew there was no mistaking what was going to happen next.

I dropped from my bike and bent over in a short-stop stance, waiting. I felt my legs tremble, then the awful heaving sensation took over. After throwing up repeatedly, I weakly swung my leg back over the center bar of my bicycle and did my best to make it the last few yards home.

I struggled with the latch on our screen door for a moment, and then stumbled into the front room loudly. I poked my head through the doorway only to find Dad mesmerized by the late edition of the sports on our local news. Mom was fast asleep on his shoulder.

"I'm home," I choked out.

"What are you doing here?" my dad asked suspiciously. I immediately wondered by I hadn't just snuck in.

"I . . . got sick."

"Wha - who's that?" Mom was waking up.

"Mike's home," Dad answered. "Do the Brazon's know that you're here?"

Oh that. "Uh, yea they do." I had almost forgotten our fool-proof plan for the night. Triton and I were hanging out at Brazon's house. And Brazon said he was over at the Triton's. Our parents didn't even call to check with each other anymore - we were always spending the night at one of the three houses. "I just told them . . . well . . . that I was sick."

". . . and you'd feel better at home." Mom finished the sentence for me. I didn't have to guess at her reaction. She jumped up and raced toward me with her fever hand outstretched for an immediate reading. "Well you aren't running a fever, but you are pale and, oh! You're wringing wet. Jack, he's broken out in a cold sweat. Make room for him on the couch and be sure he covers up. I'll go get something to settle his stomach."

Mom in action. She was a sight to behold. Any stranger would swear she was a combat nurse. She probably should have been. She'd race around in a flurry of thermometers, aspirin, cool washcloths, and warm blankets. Harsh and commanding to the healthy, she was the captain of comfort to the ill.

As I took my place on the end of the couch and burrowed beneath the thick afghan that Dad threw over me, I tried to concentrate on the weather segment. High tomorrow in the low 80's. Chance of afternoon showers. Cooler tomorrow night. Low in the mid-50's. Hints of fall. *Oh no! Football practice starts tomorrow and here I am, sick on the couch!* Even as I was thinking it, I heard the shaking bottle. No - not that! Armed with a container of pink chalk in one hand and a tablespoon in the other, Mom took her army stance directly in front of me.

"Two tablespoons of this and you'll feel better in no time. Open up now."

As I watched the thick liquid ooze out of the bottle, my stomach kicked into reverse. I barely made it to the toilet in time for a new series of heaving. Mom was right behind me, one hand locked on my forehead, the other braced on my back. I could hear her mumbling about waiting on the medicine.

"Why don't you just go on to bed and get some rest," she suggested as I quieted. "Call if you need me."

I lowered myself onto my bed and once I felt certain that my stomach wasn't going to throw me any surprises, I closed my eyes and waited for sleep. Yet the more I willed it, the further it slipped away from me. In the stillness of the night, forbidden thoughts seeped into my mind like a cold draft. I tried forcefully to push the thoughts away, but they refused to leave. I pulled the sheets up and weakly tried to straighten out the ball of covers at the end of my bed. I curled on my side beneath the twisted blankets.

I realized that nothing could give me comfort that night - not my warm bed, or Mom's pink medicine, and especially not reliving the events that I never should have witnessed to begin with. Yet it seemed inevitable that I rerun them over and over in my mind. I could shut my eyes, but I couldn't shut out the sights and sounds of that night. That was a battle I could not seem to win.

Chapter 2

I opened my eyes slowly, one eyelid at a time. A sense of gloom settled over me but I couldn't quite say why. I closed my eyes for another moment, trying to recall the nightmare that lingered. Yes, it was a nightmare. But I hadn't been sleeping. The sounds from the night before began playing over in my mind. I mopped my forehead with the back of my hand in an attempt to wipe away the memories, but the gloom wouldn't disappear.

I let my head roll to the side and tried to refocus. As my eyes settled on a dirty jersey on the floor in my bedroom, I snapped to attention. Football! Today was the first day of practice! I couldn't miss the first day of football practice.

I closed my eyes again, swallowed hard and began working out my plan. It was something I ate at the Brazon's. Brazon's mom was always fixing weird dishes, so Mom would probably buy that. But then her medical nature would possess her and demand temperature, color, throat, ears, and even my tongue.

I might pass her check-up, but the minute by minute scrutiny would be more trying. I would need just the right amount of nonchalance. No begging or pleading - that would suggest weakness. I knew I would have to play this like a master.

I sat up cautiously, realizing that if the first thing my mom saw was me racing to the toilet, the rest of my plan might as well be flushed down too. I stood slowly - so far, so good.

Nurse Rassonawski sat at her post sipping coffee when I walked in the kitchen. She rose to eye me in her professional manner, and then approached me with her fever hand outstretched and sympathetic look in place.

"How are we doing this morning?"

We? I didn't see anyone else facing this examination. "Fine, Mom." I added an authentic roll of my eyes. I only allowed a brush of her hand to my forehead as I passed by.

Following my normal morning routine, I addressed the refrigerator first. I stood with the door open, my back to Mom, checking out the possibilities for breakfast. I poked around some dishes and opened some lids keeping the fridge door open long enough to get a reaction. "Mike, shut that door!" I settled for the milk. I grabbed the carton and dropped into a chair. After twisting off the cap, I raised the jug to my open mouth. "Mike! Get a glass!" After pouring the ice-cold milk into a glass and taking a nonchalant swig, Mom started her predictable line of questions.

"You slept last night? I didn't hear you up at all."

"Yeah, fine. But I don't think I'm going to the Brazon's to eat anymore."

"Why's that?"

"His mom fixes some weird food."

"Think that's what upset your stomach?"

"Ugh. If you had seen it . . . you'd understand."

"Do you think your stomach could handle some regular home cooking?" She threw me a grin.

"I could sure use something good to eat." This was too easy!

Ten minutes later, a stack of blueberry pancakes was ceremoniously placed before me. I watched the thick maple syrup drip lazily down the edge of the stack. I grinned inwardly at how smoothly this morning had gone. *Maybe I should try out for the school play. I seem to have a great deal of talent.*

"I thought those pancakes might just bring a smile to your face!" Mom glowed with self-satisfaction.

"Oh, yeah. You know it."

Just as I stabbed the first piece, the phone rang. *Perfect timing! Now I can relax without Mom's complete attention on me.*

The patient was forgotten as Mom became engrossed in her conversation. I listened half-heartedly as I cautiously worked my way through the stack of pancakes.

"Around here? What makes them think that?" Drama. It had to be Mom's friend, Sandy. "I just couldn't believe that any of our kids . . ."

Sandy's father was the retired Chief of Police of some Chicago suburb. She had been raised listening to stories of criminals, chases, and arrests. It seemed that she had an ear for trouble, and a mouth for spreading news. At that moment she was a perfect distraction. Mom seemed intent on whatever account was being broadcast.

I finished most of my pancakes and casually stood up, cleared my plate, and set it on the counter. She glanced at me momentarily, ready to ask something, but was pulled back into Sandy's conversation. "And what should we be looking for?"

Breakfast was complete, my nonchalance applaudable, and Mom was temporarily distracted. I slipped back into my bedroom to grab my football and head outside. "Mike!" Mom held her hand over the mouthpiece of the phone, ready to stop me and finish her examination. I could feel all of my work ready to slip down the drain when my twin brothers raced into the kitchen on their Big Wheels.

"BOYS!" the command for silence followed me as I slipped out the back door. I had pulled it off! I glanced back in the kitchen through the screen door and saw Mom still on her cell, serving the twins their breakfast.

They were diving in eagerly, dodging Mom's arm as she poured their juice.

Nothing was even mentioned about football practice. Maybe she forgot all about it. At 12:30, I was in my room dressing and 10 minutes later, I left the house without so much as a questioning look.

It was too easy. Mom was preoccupied with dusting. As I mentioned where I was going, I noticed that she was deep in thought, almost entranced. She barely nodded as she stared through me. I almost asked, but decided to leave well enough alone. Maybe I shouldn't have.

Practice turned out to be more paperwork than footwork. After taking a quick count of players, we were divided up according to age. Our coach, who doubled as assistant coach to the varsity team, took charge after the division.

He handed out our practice schedule, and then delivered the customary beginning-of-the-season speech: work hard, follow directions, play as a team, and remember sportsmanship (which builds character and pride in ourselves, our team, our community, and our country). Finally, no chewing gum on the playing field.

Brazon and Triton completely ignored me for the first half of the session, threw a few side-glances and pointed looks through the pep talk, and finally brushed past me on the way to get our practice jerseys and game uniforms.

We were free to leave after storing our practice clothes in our assigned lockers and reporting the combination to the coach. Regular practice, we were informed, was to begin the next day. As I stood in line waiting for the coach to find my name on the alphabetized list, I noticed Brazon and Triton searching for their lockers.

I knew they'd be the last ones to finish. The coaches always found a way to delay Triton. As they drooled over his height and build, they would pump him for information about his skills and playing level, testing to see if his football knowledge and desire matched his physique. For as long as I could remember, John Tritle had loomed far above the rest of us. Anyone could tell that he came by his height naturally when they saw the Tritle family: six foot, seven inch father and six foot mother. But his love for the game was the real driving force behind his success. His dad was an avid sports fan and had taken special care in preparing his only son for glory days on the field.

He *was* awesome, and he knew it. And like every truly great player, he tried not to show it - usually. Oh, he thought nothing of showing who was in charge if someone crossed him, but those moments were few and far between and so out of character that it was pretty easy to swallow. Mostly, he was intense, regimented, and strategic, thus his nickname "Triton". Brazon coined it: a cross between Tritle and the great Trojan warriors. Anyway, it seemed far more fitting than his real name, Johnny.

"Hey - wait up." They were still standing in line as I reached the door.

"Yea, I'll be outside," I called back.

As I stood leaning against the rail leading to the locker room, I hurriedly thought through possible excuses for how I had acted the night before. Just the flicker of those memories made my pulse quicken. Until that moment, I had successfully pushed all undesirable thoughts from my mind, and I knew I couldn't sort through them now. I would have plenty of time for that later. Now I had to figure out how to get out of this unwanted confrontation.

"What a waste of a practice day." I heard them coming down the narrow passageway from the locker room.

"I would've just skipped it if I knew this was all we were going do." Then they rounded the corner. "Oh, you did wait." Brazon looked at me coldly. "I thought maybe you'd have to run home to Mommy and Daddy."

"Hey, I don't have to wait." I said as I walked away in a determined stride.

"Ease up," Triton ordered.

Alright. They weren't too mad, otherwise they would have let me go. I expected them to be put off, at least for awhile.

"What was with you last night?" Brazon gave me a look that told me he was still disgusted.

No, they probably wouldn't understand, or believe what I say. I felt the indecision clamp down on my chest. Why hadn't I made a plan earlier? If they knew the truth about Zeek, maybe they'd feel sorry for him and lighten up a little. Maybe we could even do something to help him. Once they found out what kind of nightmare he'd been living through, they'd *have* to understand.

Or, more likely, they'd *understand* that Zeek and I were "good buddies" - first I stuck up for him instead of sticking to their plan, and then I came up with this ridiculous story about his dad. That's what it would sound like: some story I dreamed up to save my new "buddy". After that, he probably *would* be my only friend.

"Whatsa matter, Razz? You look like you could puke," Triton acted as if the thought was making him equally sick.

That's it! "Yea, it's the flu. Got it last night."

"See?" Triton gloated to Brazon. "I told you he was sick or something."

This was the second time today that I had gotten out of a corner without trying. It was almost scary. Things never seemed to work out that easily for me.

"Then how'd you make it to practice today? Your mom would never let you come with the flu. And back off! I don't want you near me!" Brazon was still suspicious.

"I told her it was your mom's cooking that made me sick."

"Anybody'd believe that!" Triton burst out laughing.

Brazon looked like he might be offended for a moment, and then couldn't hold back himself. "And you guys are always asking why I'm so skinny! By the way, whose house am I eating at tonight?"

We were still laughing when we reached my corner.

"Wanna go throw a few?" Brazon looked at us.

"Yea, I'm in."

"Good. Then go get your football. You're closest," Triton said.

Triton, like always, was in charge. He was a natural leader. I was the brains. Brazon was the schemer: devious and manipulative with just enough edge to make him respected. We understood a little of that personality came from his home life. His dad was was in and out of work, and in and out of his life. Brazon's mom was left in charge. She was no match for Brazon's strong will and ability to bend the truth.

And there was a fourth. I couldn't help but to think of him as I ran up the back porch steps. He fit in, too. The stooge. The target. The focus of Brazon's schemes. The butt of my jokes. The slave at Triton's command. And the punching bag for his father.

Geez, how could he always act so happy? The idiotic smile was always pasted on his face, no matter what we said or did. I wondered if he wore it around his father too. Maybe that was the reason for it. Maybe his dad had slapped him around so much that it knocked something loose upstairs. My guilt ramped up a notch at the thought.

No one was home at our house, so I grabbed the football and flew out the back door.

"About time. Move like that and you'll be keeping a spot warm on the bench," Triton looked down at me with an air of authority.

"Yea, well don't you worry about it. I'll be movin' so fast that while you think you're blocking a tackle for me, I'll already be in the end zone with a big T." I tucked the ball into the crook of my arm, dodged a few imaginary tackles, and broke free for the end of the block.

Behind me I heard Brazon clapping, then shouting, "Hey - way to go! Only . . . you're in the wrong end zone!"

I could hear them cutting up behind me. It felt good to be back to normal.

We threw the football around for a half hour or so, and tried to run a few plays but realized there wasn't a whole lot that we could do with just three players. There wasn't enough time to drum up anyone else, since I had to be home before Dad got off work.

"There's our answer!" Brazon's voice shook me out of my thoughts. I acted as if I had been following their conversation all along and looked in the direction that he was staring. I knew immediately why he wore such a devious look when I made out Zeek's figure moving slowly down the street towards the empty lot where we were practicing.

Unexpectedly, the blueberry pancakes threatened. I felt them lodge at the base of my throat, refusing to let me swallow.

"It's time for everyone's favorite game," Brazon started in his announcer's voice. "What will it be today, contestants? 'Can-Mr.-Freak-Man?' or an old favorite 'Smear-the-" he stopped mid-sentence when he glanced at me.

He was going to be short one contestant. Shortstop position. *Oh no. Not now!* I pleaded under my breath. But my stomach had turned on me and refused to be reasoned with.

"Hey Razz. You okay?" I could hear Triton behind me.

The best I could do was shake my head. I could hear Brazon walking over. "He's gonna puke. Oh man. Not here! Not in the middle of the field."

Too late. Everybody stand back. Showtime.

After I had left my mark in the middle of our practice field, I weakly commented that I must have pushed it too much and I was gonna just go home.

"Yea. We might as well go, too. I'm not about to fall in that pile of . . . of . . ." Brazon looked disgusted.

"Let's just go," Triton interrupted, leaving Zeek's lonely outline forgotten in the distance.

Brazon and Triton kept a cautious eye on me all the way to my house. I knew what they were afraid of, and I didn't blame them. Still, I felt much better now.

I was ready to say as much when Brazon blurted out, "Well, you saved your good buddy Zeeky again. Seems like you're always coming to his rescue."

His comment was directed towards me, but before I could defend myself, that same nauseous feeling took me by surprise and oozed up my throat. My look must have betrayed me, because Brazon shot me an unexpected shove that nearly left me face down.

"Geez! Go over in the grass if you're gonna . . ."

"I'm fine!" I interrupted in a snide tone that told him I didn't appreciate his helpfulness. "I'll see you guys tomorrow at practice." I turned and walked towards my house without waiting for a reply.

If only I hadn't been there to see what had happened. If only I could quit reliving it over and over again.

I knew I had to do something, and I had to do it soon. I couldn't stay like this. After all, I had football practice tomorrow. Real practice. I couldn't go through that feeling like someone was twisting my stomach until it was completely wrung out. I had to think of something fast.

I sat on the front step of our porch. I knew that I couldn't tell Brazon and Triton the whole story. They obviously didn't want to listen. Maybe I could tell Zeek what I knew, and then we could turn his dad in to the authorities. No, something told me that if Zeek had hidden the truth for that long, he was not going to be too eager to come forward with it now.

Then an idea began to form. Maybe an answer. It was simple. Logical. Easy. And good for everyone. I would just be nice to the guy. Actually, talk to him. Be his friend - as long as Brazon and Triton weren't around. Yea, he needed a friend. It'd make him feel good to think we were, well, kind of buddies.

Just making the decision was a relief. I wouldn't lose my old friends over the whole deal if I played it right. And I wouldn't have to feel guilty anymore.

However, I soon found out that there are worse things than a little quilt.

Chapter 3

Our junior high was a newly formed consolidation of Milton and our two neighboring towns, Sparta and Rockton. Sparton Junior High. This recent merge brought unexpected opportunities. Better school. Better teams. Better equipment. But most importantly - better girls.

Now, I had never really been one to complain about our selection while I was in elementary school. But then, I was only a kid and I really had nothing to compare it with. We had gone to school with the same group of kids from day one. And girls absolutely took a back seat to football or hanging around with my buddies.

But that was before. Now I had the chance to see the benefits of a consolidation. None of us would argue that it was a worthwhile venture, even though our town fought the hardest against consolidation.

Our parents' big fear was what effect the students from those larger schools would have on our innocent hometown kids. Rumors ran rampant about problems with drugs and alcohol that would assuredly accompany any connection with those particular towns.

However, our school simply had no funds to function another year. There didn't seem to be another alternative. And on that first day of school, I was thanking our school's deficit as I watched one particular girl step down from her bus.

Her long, black hair was blowing away from her face. The sunlight reflected her perfectly tanned skin and when her eyes met mine - those deep, brown eyes - I knew this was it. Unfortunately, the bell rang and that *was* it. She might need a little convincing that I was a prize worthy of her time, but I was sure I knew just how to do it.

We only had two classes together, which was enough time to learn that her name was Maria, but not enough time to persuade her that a catch like me as a once-in-a-lifetime opportunity. Especially since all I could manage to do was stare at her. And the teachers were not helping in my endeavor.

"Mr. Rassonawski must think that Miss Roberts has the answer written somewhere upon her person." Impressive. Very impressive. I knew Maria was impressed when she turned three shades of red. This was not the way to score points with her. At this rate, I could imagine that I would die a lonely old man.

But I had a plan. Football. All girls were impressed with football players, and I knew that she would fall for me when she saw me on the starting line-up of our team. In the weeks of practice before school had started, I thought of nothing else. I arrived at the daily practices early and stayed late. While my teammates were showering and slamming locker doors, exhausted from a tough day of practice, I was still on the field running the play routes over and over, blocking imaginary defensive players, making it into the end zone each time. I showed up in the weight-lifting room with the dedication of an Iron Man trainee. While others put on a show of lifting at each station; I huffed and puffed, lifted and squatted, ignoring the normal banter among my friends. I was on a mission. I had my mind fixed on earning a starting position on our offensive line, and I knew without a doubt that I would be there. Now it was time to apply that same determination to a new goal: Maria Roberts.

In the meantime, I needed to rethink my plan for helping Zeek because of an unexpected twist.

Within days, he was following me around like a lost puppy. He wouldn't say much, he was just this silent presence. Between classes when I switched out my books, I would slam my locker door shut and BAM, there he was. I would walk out of the bathroom and he'd be standing there waiting for me. In study hall, he would angle his way over from his normal corner seat to get closer to my table. He couldn't seem to get it through his thick skull that although I felt sorry for him and all, I couldn't ruin my life and friendships over the whole thing. I mean, how hard was it to figure out that I was trying to be friendly to him, but only in private?

He had acted surprised, even suspicious, with my first few efforts to be civil. I couldn't really blame him. I had never seen anyone act genuinely nice to him before. As I thought about it, I convinced myself I was going to make this guy's life worth living.

I carefully selected times when I could stay after PE for a minute or two, so we'd be the only ones in the locker room. Then I'd try to casually make small talk. At first it was so awkward. I mean, it was strange to actually talk *to* Zeek. We were all used to talking about him, or shouting things at him, or getting in our last dig before he walked away. But we never really talked *to* the guy.

The first time I tried, he completely ignored me. He must've thought there was someone else in the locker room with us, because when he turned away from his locker to leave, he looked around, obviously confused. Then with a stunned expression, he cautiously asked if I was talking to him.

"Yea. I said ya did alright out there today."

He stood there staring at me like *I* was the circus freak. It was like he'd never gotten a compliment before. I didn't say anything more. I left him standing there, gaping like a guy who'd just won a million dollars. I felt rather proud of myself for throwing him such a bone and decided it was best not to dish out too much at one time. I was scared to think of how he might react.

Later that week I tried again. Passing in the hallway, I threw him a glance and nod and walked on. For some reason, after that acknowledgement, Zeek seemed to think that he couldn't let me out of his sight. Like he owed me something, and he was going to follow me around until he paid me back.

This became a problem as I inconspicuously tried to keep Maria in my sight. There was nothing inconspicuous about the fact that every time I got close to her, I'd look over my shoulder and see Zeek hovering in the background. No girl was going to want me around if I was being followed by a geek with a bug-eyed stare locked on me.

Brazon and Triton actually seemed to relish the fact that the target of their pranks stayed so close. If they thought it was weird, they never mentioned it. They were too busy thinking of new jabs and stunts to toss at their stooge. Zeek took it good-naturedly. He would laugh along, though his laugh seemed strained and hesitant. I caught several of his questioning glances to see if I was joining in. It was a tough tightrope walk that I was performing, staying on the side of my friends, while trying to befriend the one who truly needed it. I was pretty confident that God was pleased with my efforts.

My next opportunity came a couple of days later when I noticed Zeek walking home alone from school. Brazon and Triton both had detention that night for being late to English. The coast was clear.

I waited until we were several blocks from school. I watched Zeek as he unknowingly trudged along. After checking and rechecking to be sure that no one was within seeing or hearing distance, I casually called out to him.

He spun around, surprised. "Me?"

What a stupid question. I couldn't resist. "No, the Zeek behind you." Predictably, he looked over his left shoulder.

Suddenly embarrassed, he looked down at his feet. "Oh."

"Wait up."

His expression suddenly changed to one of a kid's in a candy store after he had just been handed a dollar bill. It was like this was the greatest thrill of his lifetime - to have me walk home with him. It was a real kick to have so much power over a person. All I needed to do was snap my fingers and make his day. It felt great to be so important.

I strutted up to him with an air of importance and graced him with a few words. "Coming to the game tonight?" I tried to look somewhat interested.

"No, I can't." He looked genuinely disappointed.

"Why not?"

"My dad's . . . " he stopped himself. I could almost see him work through the possible excuses, trying to find one that sounded realistic. ". . . uh, my dad's got something for me to do tonight."

"Oh," I said, playing along, "well, just do it early, then you can come. We don't play til 6:00."

"Uhh . . ." I had thrown him a curveball. I watched as the wheels turned in his mind and he figured out a new excuse.

"Well, see what you can do," I graciously let him off the hook and started walking.

"Yea, okay. I will." His concentrated look melted away and was replaced by his predictable idiotic smile. "Yea," he repeated, "I'll see what I can do."

I wondered what was such a big deal about admitting that he was grounded. I mean, it happened to all of us. Brazon even bragged about how many times a month he'd get grounded. I didn't go that far, but I sure didn't let it bother me. Well, I figured everybody had their own quirks. Then with an inward grin I added to myself, *even if Zeek has more than his fair share.*

An uncomfortable silence settled between us, and I was relieved to see my street coming up. When we reached the corner, we stopped and looked at each other a minute. Zeek tugged at his heavy jacket and ran a finger around the turtleneck that hugged his chin.

There was a fine example of one of his oddities. He'd wear clothes that looked like he had a paranoid grandmother dressing him. Seventy-five degrees out and he was wearing a turtleneck, heavy corduroys, and a jacket. He had to be sweating!

"So, maybe I will see you tonight," he said as if calculating the possibility.

"Yea, we'll see."

"6:00 you said? That's kick-off then?"

"Right. I gotta go."

"Hey - wait," he was searching. "I don't really want to go home yet. Wanna go throw the football around?"

"Well . . ." I quickly began to calculate the time. I had hung around after school, hoping to see Maria before she got on the bus. Once I saw Zeek, I took my dear sweet time making sure all was clear before I called him. Then we plodded along, Zeek-style, to the corner. I had a feeling that I had let this whole thing go a little too far.

I was right. If only I could have erased the last few minutes and cut to my house as soon as we hit the corner, I would've been home free. I could have saved myself a world of trouble, along with Zeek.

"Ah-ah-ah . . . what have we here?" I recognized his voice from a block away, even before I could see his face. "Our good buddies talking over their plans before the big game?" He was including me in that same sarcastic tone that was usually directed exclusively at Zeek. A nasty feeling crawled into my stomach. I didn't like this. Not a bit.

Before I had a chance to explain, Triton took his shot at Zeek. "Hey, we're low on dummies for tackle practice. Wanna volunteer, Zeekman?"

"Sure," Zeek answered easily enough. I noticed his blank look had reappeared. It seemed he could slip into that look as easily as he put on a cap.

I jumped in without missing a beat. "Naw - you don't want him. The dummy would be more of a challenge."

A chuckle and look of approval crossed Triton's face. Zeek shot a quick look of confusion my way, but quickly recovered with a half-grin. However, Brazon still wasn't convinced.

"What are ya doing, Razz? Protecting your new buddy again?"

"From what?" I had to throw it back to him. "You couldn't hit hard enough to even knock a dummy down. You don't need Zeek in there, the dummies walk away laughing at your hits."

Our normal, demeaning digs were working. Triton was nearly bent over laughing, but a glance at Brazon told me he wouldn't give up so easily.

"Hey," he directed his bladed look towards me, "at least I hit 'em. I don't hang around with them."

It was time to save face. My charity work was done for the day. After all, I had done Zeek enough favors, now I had to get back in with my friends.

"Whatdaya mean - hang around with 'em? I was just on my way home when he caught up to me and then started begging me to play catch. I thought I could use a good laugh, so I was thinking about it." Then a direct challenge to Brazon, "You got a problem with that?" The lie had come too easily. I stared defiantly at my friends, as if I had every right to defend my dignity.

"No, but I think *you* do. Everybody's noticed how you and Zeeky have been buddy-buddy these past few days. Geez, the guy's glued to you like fly paper. What's the deal?"

"You think we're . . . friends? Get real." I glanced over at him with a look of aversion to complete my act, but what I saw in his eyes made me freeze.

Hurt. Betrayal. Even a little anger. He didn't say a word. He just walked away, head down and shoulders slumped.

So much for good intentions. I wanted to help, to make things better for Zeek. All I succeeded in doing was doubling the problem. *Lord, what have I done? The guy doesn't have any friends, his home should be condemned, his father should be put away for mistreating him, and You called me to help. Now I just stabbed him in the back.*

I didn't even notice Brazon and Triton staring at me. I couldn't take my eyes off of Zeek's solitary outline in the distance. *I should go. I should tell him - explain. Apologize. Help.* Help? That was a laugh. I had "helped" enough already. I was losing my balance on the tightrope.

"Seems like ole' Zeek didn't get the joke," Brazon smirked.

"Shut up, you idiot," I hissed with all the venom I felt for myself.

"What the . . . "

I didn't give him time to finish. I turned on my heels and stormed home in long, deliberate strides. Just as I reached my porch, I heard them catching up behind me.

"Razz!" Triton's commanding voice told me I'd better acknowledge him. I turned around slowly and let a smoldering glare settle on the two of them.

Triton seemed confused and taken aback. Brazon matched my look with his ever-popular smirk. "What's the deal, Rassonawski?" he sneered. "You turned into a freak-lover?"

"I don't need to listen to this. Get outta here." My anger broke free as I laid into Brazon with a half-push, half-jab that landed squarely in the center of his chest. He stumbled backwards, caught unaware.

Confident that I had made my message clear, I once again turned to go inside. I didn't see Brazon's foot as he tucked it quickly and smoothly in front of mine. My reflexes kicked in before I even knew what was happening. Although I landed face-down on the hard pavement, my hands were there first, faithfully breaking my fall.

I found myself inspecting a single brown pebble trapped in the cement as I debated my next move. I knew what I wanted to do, and what I felt like doing, but I also knew what I should do.

I lifted myself slowly to my feet, deliberately keeping my back to my two best friends. I brushed off my hands slowly, allowing myself a few more seconds to make a decision. Then without further thought, I continued my previous path as if nothing had happened. Better no decision than the wrong decision.

"Hey!" Triton demanded. Still I didn't turn around. Then suddenly he was blocking my way, with one very imposing finger poking me in the chest. "What's going on? You've got some explaining to do."

"Yea, right." I threw in a daring move, slapping his jab away from my chest. "Just back off."

Something in my attitude must have set him back; otherwise I would have regretted that move. Realizing that I had tempted fate about as much as I should, I eased up slightly.

"C'mon," I ordered evenly as I brushed past them to the back steps of my porch. "Let's go inside."

Mom was in the kitchen worrying over steaming pans with Barry and Terry, each sitting on their "naughty stools." It wasn't difficult to figure out the story behind their so-called punishment after just a quick glance at their teary eyes, tousled hair, and angry looks. It was also plain to see that their three-year-old minds were not thinking about the misbehavior as they were supposed to. Their steamy looks at each other behind Mom's back made it obvious that their thoughts were more centered on how to get revenge when their time was up.

We slipped past the scene with a quick acknowledgement from Mom, but unnoticed by the twins. "In here," I motioned toward my room.

As I shut the door, I was overcome by the possibility that this plan was going to backfire, just as all of my other ones had so far.

"So what's the big deal?" pressed Triton impatiently.

Brazon had settled on the back corner of my bed, slumped comfortably into his normal position against the wall with one foot dangling to the side of the bed and one outstretched, nearly resting on my pillow. He was tossing the football casually into the air, obviously determined not to buy any of my explanations before I even started.

I made a mental note to focus my concentration on Triton. He was more likely to believe and accept my story, as well as the reasoning behind what I did. Besides, I knew a secret about Triton that I felt certain no one else knew. He had a soft spot. It was very well hidden, and he took great care to keep it private. But I had seen it once when we were at Triton's house playing a typical game of football.

Brazon had thrown a wild pass over the roof of the house, and it bounced into the front driveway. Triton raced off to retrieve it, throwing sarcastic remarks over his shoulder about Brazon's ability, or more accurately, his lack of it. He was gone for quite awhile. Brazon shot me a questioning look. For lack of anything better to do, I charged off to see what was taking so long. As I rounded the garage corner, I froze instantly as I encountered the unexpected scene before me.

Triton was down on one knee with his other leg balanced off to the side, creating a bench for his little sister, Trisha. He had her cradled in his arm, with his other hand stroking her long silky hair and occasionally brushing away a stray tear. From the dirt on her leg and backside, it was apparent that she had somehow fallen and was now recovering with the help of her comforting big brother. I snuck back behind the garage before being discovered.

I had never mentioned that scene to anyone, especially Triton. But I knew. And I hoped that somehow Zeek might find a piece of that hidden soft spot.

Unlike Brazon, the youngest of four boys. With him I had never seen even a glimmer of understanding or empathy. Oh, he knew how to play the game with our parents, who actually believed that his polite manners reflected his character. I knew better. He was raised tough, especially by the older brothers who had now moved out of the house. The only brother left living at home basically ignored him. If they exchanged words, the harshness and cruelty made me cringe.

I tried not thinking of him at all, sitting there on my bed with a smug look imprinted on his face. I dismissed him with a glance and purposely turned my back to his corner.

"We ain't got all day," Triton led my explanation impatiently.

Don't start off on the wrong foot, I reminded myself.

"I know. I'm getting to it." Still unsure of myself, I dove in. "The night we had Zeek on the bin . . . "

"We?" I heard Brazon echo sarcastically from his corner. "We? If I recall, you were *bored* with the whole deal. There was no *we* about it."

"Anyway," I interrupted without even turning around or giving him a second look, "that night I saw something."

"Oh, let me guess," I turned around to find Brazon's actions matching his tone. He pinched a finger and thumb against the bridge of his nose with his eyes squeezed tightly shut as if he were thinking. I wasn't about to give him time to finish mocking me. I turned around again quickly.

"It was at Zeek's house," I continued.

"Oh? You went to Zeek's place? Did you girls have a nice time?" Brazon wasn't quitting yet. I knew that he hated being ignored, so that is exactly what I intended to do.

"I hung out by the front of his house, watching his old man. He was wild - crazy wild. Not just drunk, but scary, you know? I mean mad. It freaked me out just to be there watching."

"So what's new? He's always been a goon."

"Like father, like son," chimed in Brazon.

"Just shut up and listen." I saw Triton stiffen and knew instantly that I had put him off. I'd have to watch it if I wanted him to take my side. I started again, this time more slowly. "His dad was pounding on stuff and kicking junk around the house and yelling about being mad at Zeek. You could hear him swearing all the way down the block. He was hot.

"I figured he was just mad about Zeek being late and all, so I was ready to take off, but then Zeek came home."

"Boys? Boys! Dinner's ready in ten minutes. Are you boys eating here tonight?"

"No, Mrs. R. Thanks anyway, but we've got to get ready for the game tonight." Suddenly Brazon was Mr. Polite.

"Well, you boys are sure welcome to stay. Mike, I want you out here in ten minutes."

"Yea, Mom. Alright." I shouted back to her. Then in a more hushed tone, "So anyway," I looked up and noticed that I had Triton's complete attention. Good. "So anyway, he tried to sneak in the back so his dad wouldn't catch him . . . you know." I had to stop a minute. I could feel the burn rise from the bottom of my throat. I swallowed, trying to force it back down.

"That's it?" Triton looked confused and was obviously losing his patience.

"No. I wish it was." I took a slow breath and went on. "I could hear Old Man Zeekman getting madder and madder, and then he started pounding on the table. Zeek must have figured he'd been caught, cause the next thing I know, Zeek was racing upstairs. Then I heard his door slam shut."

"Yea, yea, yea. Get to the point, huh? I gotta get going," Brazon's sarcastic tone had turned cold, and I suddenly wished he would just leave.

But I didn't let him get to me. "Old Man Zeekman must have heard him too cause next thing I knew, he was upstairs using Zeek as a punching bag. And I don't mean just slapping him around a little. I mean - doing some serious damage."

"How do you know? Don't tell me you could see what happened in Zeek's room." Triton looked suspicious.

"I could hear . . ."

A suffocating silence fell on the room. Suddenly, Brazon sliced through it with his cutting words. "Razz, you're dumber than I thought. You think we're idiots, too? If his dad was beating on him like you say, why haven't any of us seen any bruises? Or cuts? Huh? Get a clue. All you probably heard was his dad beating on some furniture. That's about all the smarts he's got. But I figured you had more."

"You weren't there." I turned to Triton. I could see that Brazon's comments were swaying Triton's opinion quicker than I could. And yet, he *did* have a point. But I wasn't ready to concede. "Hey, I haven't been looking for any bruises, have you?" Even as I was saying it, I began doubting my conclusion for the same reason. Somebody should've seen bruises by now. A slice of hope shot through me. Maybe I was wrong. Maybe . . . but then I replayed the sounds of that night, and I knew better.

Brazon just shrugged off my question.

Triton jumped in. "Why would the guy beat Zeek just for being a little late? That doesn't make sense."

"Hey, who could explain that guy?" Then a piece of the night flipped to the front of my thoughts. There was something else. "Old Man Zeekman was yelling about making money, about Zeek doing his part. I don't know," I knew it wasn't making sense. "Maybe Zeek was supposed to be working or doing something else that night. He was awful worried about getting home on time."

"Mi-ke!" Mom's perfect timing hit again. "Dinner's ready - NOW! Remember, you have a game tonight!"

"One minute, Mom."

"No! Not one minute! NOW!"

"Listen, I gotta go anyway." Triton was headed for the door.

"Quit trying to make somethin' out of nothin'." Brazon shot in.

"But you weren't there. You don't know."

"Yea, we do know." Brazon's look suddenly changed to a smirk. "And I don't think your little Maria would want anything to do with a freak-lover."

"She isn't *my* Maria."

"You're right. And I might just make her *mine.* I'd hate to see Zeek's best buddy chasing after her. Poor girl might get a bad reputation from that." And then with even more emphasis, "I mean it, Razz. Give it up." And they were gone.

If I could have given it up, I would have. But something inside of me wouldn't let it go - couldn't forget. I wished I could just turn it off. But now, especially now, I knew that was impossible. Worse yet, I had a feeling that I was going to face this thing alone.

Chapter 4

Bruises. I woke up thinking about them. And feeling them. The game was rough, like the rest of the day had been. Extra points at the buzzer. We almost blocked their kick, but *almost* never won a game. Triton played like a madman. I saw the varsity coach pull him aside after the game. Our fears were finally materializing - we were going to lose him to the varsity team. Brazon warmed the bench for half of the game after starting a fight with their tackle and yelling at the official.

I was in most of the time, running the routes that I had practiced so diligently. But somehow I ended up on the bottom of things - literally. Facing up to a linebacker bent on pulverizing the opposition, I was bound to end up on my backside more times than I could count. But I held my own for the most important plays, one of which allowed Kurt, our quarterback, to sneak into the end zone. He was rewarded with cheers and pats, while I got smashed by Mr. Massive who was less than impressed with being pushed aside momentarily. After the game, everyone rushed to encourage Kurt and assure him of a win the next time. I hit the locker without being noticed.

There was one glimmer of hope when I thought that I had caught Maria's eye as she strode onto the field with the other cheerleaders. I had, but it was only by accident. She ran past me and when I turned to let my gaze follow her, I found her cornered by Brazon, who was undoubtedly staying true to his word.

Well he could have her. What'd I need with a stupid girlfriend anyhow? Girls just got in a guy's way - always wanting attention when I had better things to do, like be with my buddies. I turned from my thoughts to grab just one more glimpse and found them walking away together. *Yea. Some buddy.*

I walked off the field thinking that nothing else could go wrong that night, but there was time for just one more disaster.

I had showered quickly, just wanting to get home, hit the bed and finish the horrible day. Mom and Dad offered to wait around after the game to drive me home, but I wanted to walk home alone. The last thing I needed was my dad's instant replays of the entire game complete with criticisms of my mistakes and sound advice for improving my game. Yeah, I could easily skip that.

I found myself shuffling along the side of the road, in no hurry to get home. The night air had a chilly bite to it but felt good. I left my coat unzipped and let the chill hit my damp T-shirt. For some reason, the coldness seemed to clear my mind and that was what I needed most.

For the first time in days, I paused long enough to think back over the events of the past month. I asked God to show me what I was supposed to be doing and asked Him to direct me, admitting that on my own I had made a real mess of things. I confessed my selfishness and poured out my regret when I remembered Zeek's hurt look that afternoon. Suddenly, all the confusion and aggravation from the day's events dissipated and the truly important issue became crystal clear: this was all about Zeek. Not me. Not my friends. Not what others thought. Not any great plan I could cook up. This *had* to be about what was best for Zeek. And so far, I was not on that list.

I slowed my pace and deepened my concentration. Rerunning scenes from that afternoon, I realized that Brazon and Triton did have a point about the bruises. How could anyone find any bruises when he was always wearing winter clothes? There were times that he didn't even take off his turtleneck for P.E. No wonder no one had ever seen any bruises. Then I knew: being a fashion statement was the least of Zeek's concerns. He very purposefully chose his wardrobe. Stupid? No. Concealing? Absolutely.

The pieces were starting to fall into place. There were days that Zeek would plead feeling sick to get out of P.E. when we all knew he was really okay. We all thought he was tired of us harassing him, but now I knew the truth. The abuse we'd give him during a game of flag football was nothing compared to the real abuse that awaited him at home.

My thoughts were directing my footsteps, and I found myself once again facing the kitchen window of the Zeekman house, only this time from the other side street. There were no trees to hide behind on this side of the road, so I slowed my steps even more in an effort to look nonchalant as I spied on the house.

Through the open side window in the kitchen, I could see several people seated around the kitchen table, heads bent, seemingly in deep discussion. Yet only quiet, muffled sounds could be heard drifting from the open window. Old Man Zeekman's unmistakable outline shifted uneasily as he stood beside the table, obviously only an onlooker to the conference going on.

I wondered at the oddness of the Zeekmans having guests at their home. The vision of Old Man Zeekman entertaining company seemed ironic, yet here they were.

"Son!" The gruff voice of Zeek's dad was the first sound that was clearly transmitted through the still night air. "Get in here now, boy."

I suddenly had to exhale as I realized I had been holding my breath.

"I told ya once, the kid ain't gonna screw it up again," he shouted. Then grabbing Zeek by the arm, he added harshly, "Are ya boy? Not after that 'little talk' we had, eh?" Zeek wagged his head obediently. Old Man Zeekman collected something from the table and pushed it at Zeek. In a voice soaked with reproach he warned, "Ya best get it right, or you'll be twice as sorry. Got it?" Then he roughly grabbed Zeek by his coat collar and shoved him out the door.

I suddenly felt as exposed as a quarterback out of his pocket with no blockers in sight. I had to get out of there. And something told me instinctively not to attempt a casual exit. I didn't spend even a moment debating the thought. In a split second, I had turned on my heel and raced down the silent, empty street.

I didn't stop running until I was well out of sight and breath. Even when my steps slowed and my breathing evened out, my mind raced at full speed. *Who were they? Why were they at Zeek's house? What was so serious? And what had Zeek screwed up?*

My mind was still in high gear as I hit the back door, but luckily my brain switched to quickly assess the situation and steer my feet away from the TV room. The inevitable critiquing of my performance in tonight's game was the last thing I needed at the moment.

I could see Mom in the kitchen on her cell. Her animated features reminded me of some of the acting I'd seen on her stupid dramas. I wondered at what gossip was keeping her so engrossed. But I was careful to sneak into my room before a break in the conversation. I wasn't up for more drama.

I was busy tossing junk from my bed in an effort to find my sheet and pillows when I was interrupted by a familiar tone of voice that told me I was in trouble.

"Mike! Mike? Where are you? Get out here." Mom's rampage voice.

A slight panic set in. What had I done? It was always best to be prepared, at least have some idea of where I had made my mistake. But, try as I might, I couldn't imagine what I had done this time. I hated going into the fight blind.

"What?"

"Where were you tonight?"

"Huh?" Caught totally off guard, I answered honestly. "At the game."

"And after the game?"

"What?"

"Just now, after the game?"

"I walked home." As I stared blankly at her accusing eyes, I quickly ran through all possible scenarios. How could I find out what was wrong? Although, judging from her voice and battle-stance, it wouldn't matter if I did know the details.

"Were you with that Jeff Zeekman at all?"

Whoa! Where is that coming from? "With who?" Again with the ignorance act to buy some time.

"That Zeekman kid. You know - the one in your class."

I didn't think she knew Zeek, certainly not well enough to be worried about how much time I spent with him. "No, I didn't see him tonight. Since when did you start worrying about my friends?"

"I'm not worried about your friends. I'm worrying about you. It's just, well it's just that . . ." Suddenly behind the stern look that controlled her face, I caught a glimpse of a frightened look.

". . . I just don't want you anywhere near that boy." She placed her hands squarely on the table, and with a meaningful squint of her eyes, she added, "Do you understand that?"

"Yeah, but why? What's the big deal about Zeek?"

"He's nothing but trouble. That's all you need to know."

Case closed. She had placed a silent, undeniable period at the end of that sentence, and from past experience I knew that I wouldn't be able to erase it.

So there I was with direct orders from my mom and friends to stay away from Zeek, but with even more persistent orders from inside of me trying to persuade me to befriend him. I now had the perfect excuse to abandon this anti-productive mission I was on. Mom didn't seem to leave me many options. Maybe this was a sign or something. I should just drop the whole thing. That would be the easiest thing to do. Eventually Brazon and Triton would forget that I'd ever brought the topic up. Yea, it would be best for everyone if I just gave up this crusade for Zeek. The more I thought about it, the more I tried to convince myself that forgetting the whole mess was the right thing to do.

But when I paused for the slightest moment, the words came to me: *it may not be easy, but it will be the right thing to do.* This time I stopped myself purposefully. I was not going to charge ahead with my own plan again or choose the easiest way out. This time I was determined to follow.

Chapter 5

Sunday morning. Mom began her normal rant. "This is the third time I've been in here to wake you up. We're going to be late! If I have to come in here again, you're going to be sorry." Bla-bla-bla. I'd heard it all before, and I knew that I had another ten minutes in bed, during which she'd try to get the twins dressed, remind Dad that he wore the same tie last Sunday, and furiously whip up the French toast batter before she noticed I wasn't moving. I knew when the sound of the whisk stopped, I had better be making some noise of my own.

I really wished she would just let me sleep this one Sunday. Maybe I could fake being sick. No, I had tried that one too many times. Maybe I could . . . just get up.

But I wasn't about to open the door to conversation, especially if it concerned Zeek. I had decided last night after her warnings that Mom was way off base on that subject. The way she talked about him made him sound like a criminal. The way she grilled me made me sound like his accomplice. I just had to remind myself that she had been watching too many reality shows lately. Maybe she had nothing better to do than to create drama in our doldrum little town. What really baffled me, though, was why she chose Zeek as the main character.

There wasn't much I could do about being stuck in this little melodrama, but I wasn't going to play an enthusiastic part. She could lay down the law and try to set the rules about Zeek, but none of it would make me stop remembering. Nothing could.

I was throwing on the only jeans that Mom would let pass on a Sunday morning when she glared in to check on me. "It's about time. Breakfast is ready. If you could hurry a little, we might make it on time this week."

The taste of the homemade French toast lingered as the church sang the opening hymn that Sunday morning. My hymnal was turned to the correct page and I obediently pretended to follow along. The twins were strategically placed on either side of Dad, which unfortunately, left me next to Mom.

I had learned early on that sitting beside Mom was the last place I wanted to be on a Sunday morning, especially if I was prone to letting my mind wander. The moment she would notice the slightest wavering of my attention, I would feel a sharp jab in my midsection, followed by her nod in the minister's direction. It didn't take too many Sundays to figure out that if I just kept my stare locked on Reverend Jamison, I could let my mind wander and my ribs not suffer.

Scenes from the past school year flashed in my mind. I could pull them up as if they happened yesterday: spitballs we aimed at the teacher, then unanimously blamed on Zeek. Or the "Kick Me" signs we'd secretly attach to his back with what he thought was a friendly pat. And then, of course, he was the garbage plate for the lunch food we didn't want, so we'd be free to get seconds of our choice.

He always seemed to be more than happy to collect our papers, sharpen our pencils, grab our books, anything we demanded for that matter. Maybe that was because it was the only way he'd ever been treated. I convinced myself that it was just harmless fun, that it didn't bother him because he was such a good sport about it all. But somewhere buried deep, I knew the truth. It was just easier to pretend I didn't.

My thoughts swirled around when suddenly a clear message rang out. "Every one of them betrayed Him. None were strong enough to stand by His side. And they knew without a doubt - He was worthy of their loyalty." It was Reverend Jamison's sermon.

I felt as if he had been audience to the scenes playing in my mind and was providing me with the answer I so desperately sought. Was it just coincidence that the solution came to me so clearly at the exact time I was seeking it? Or was the unmistakable answer given to me by the only One who could know my thoughts and could interject the answer with lightning-bolt clarity?

"All of his followers took the easy way out. Why? Because they were afraid; afraid to stand up for what they knew was right." His words were like a sledgehammer crushing each of my excuses and pounding out the truth. "And how many of us are afraid today? How many of us are willing to do what is right, no matter the cost? How many of us would stand by Jesus today?" Our eyes met briefly as Reverend Jamison scanned the congregation for the answer.

"Of course, all of us *say* we'd stand by Him, bear our cross and follow Him. But would we? Do we?" Suddenly, for what seemed a moment frozen in time, his eyes locked on mine and he added, "For didn't Jesus say that whatsoever you do for the least of them, you also do for Me?"

I knew that my questions had been heard and clear direction given. I had never had such deep conviction that washed away all doubts. My gut feeling from the very beginning had been right. Zeek needed me, and I wouldn't turn my back on him again, no matter how hard that promise would be to follow through with.

I was still marveling at my unexpected revelation through Sunday dinner. After changing into my comfortably worn T-shirt and gym shorts, I grabbed my football and headed out the door with no particular destination in mind. I wandered slowly down my block feeling confident in my decision, yet trying to form a new plan to action to befriend Zeek. *Befriend Zeek?* The thought still seemed so crazy. Just a month ago, I was playing right along with Brazon and Triton, making Zeek the object of our pranks and getting a good laugh out of it all.

Even as I was thinking it, I happened upon the scene that would be a turning point I will never forget. I rounded the corner to the empty lot where we usually practiced our passes, hiking, punting, and tackles. I could see Brazon and Triton's outlines at the opposite end of the open lot. There were a couple of other younger guys practicing with them - and Zeek.

At first it seemed like an innocent enough scrimmage, until I realized that there were no teams: only four guys and Zeek. They'd pass Zeek the ball, and then race to see who could tackle him first. Then they'd let him quarterback the ball and crush him before he could even get out of the hike stance. Every play was followed by laughs and pats on the back and Zeek trying to pick himself up quickly, acting like he wasn't hurt. At one point they sent him out on a long pass which looked like he might catch, until I noticed Brazon's foot swing out deftly in his path. The only thing he caught was a mouthful of turf and more raucous laughter.

I couldn't watch any longer. Zeek had taken enough abuse in his life without these extra helpings. A rogue thought crossed my mind that I could slip away unnoticed, as no one seemed to know I was there. But not this time. I had to take a stand. The answer that had come to me so clearly just that morning refused to be silenced. I had to do what was right, and I had to do it now.

Without thinking, I felt my feet pounding the ground as I raced across the empty lot like a madman. My thoughts of Zeek's unfair life, as well as my own self-resentment for having been a part of his pain propelled me.

As I reached the middle of the field, I saw Brazon extend a hand to help Zeek up. Zeek grasped it gladly, but just as he was raising himself up from the ground, Brazon flipped his hand free, causing Zeek to fall back awkwardly. That was the final blow. I pumped my arms faster and felt my legs extend the length of each stride. I had built my speed up to its peak when I reached Brazon from behind with both arms stretched out straight in front of me. He went flying several feet before he even knew what hit him. The force from the impact sent me tumbling forward also.

I was on my feet instantly and caught only side glances of confusion between Triton and the other players. I left them bewildered, obviously trying to decide whether I was taking my part in the game or whether it was something more. They would know soon enough.

In a second, I was on Brazon's back, pulling his scrawny arm behind him and twisting it upward in an unmistakable motion that told him this was no game. "I tried to tell you before . . ." I hissed between clenched teeth and tightened my grip to inch his arm upward. A gasp escaped him. "Zeek's got enough problems." Then with an added twist for emphasis, "Leave him alone."

Brazon lifted his head up enough to squeak out, "Tri-ton!"

That was the only word he could have uttered that burned a hole of fear in my gut. I didn't loosen my grip as I heard Triton stride up behind us.

"What's this?" I heard anger drip from his voice as I felt his iron grip around the back of my neck. "I thought we settled this earlier." He applied pressure, which I knew would intensify until I released Brazon. Triton continued his pincer hold as he guided me upward to a standing position and increased the strength of his grip.

Triton and I had never really crossed, and I had always felt a closer friendship with him than Brazon. He had always been in awe of my intelligence, and I of his strength. I decided to play on that.

"Listen. When have I ever been wrong? Trust me, I'm right on this."

I felt his grip loosen slightly, then tightened immediately as a thought struck. "It isn't my problem either way."

"True, but it isn't right to make things worse." I could feel his grip loosen again and began to feel confident that maybe I was getting through to him, that maybe I could convince him - when I caught the blurred motion of Brazon as he jumped to his feet to even the score.

Before I could react, I felt the air exploding from me as his punch seemed to crush my lungs. As I doubled over and broke Triton's grip, I felt a solid fist crush the bridge of my nose and smash the corner of my eye. I jerked my head to stare, stunned for a moment, long enough to see Brazon rubbing his fist. Then my knees buckled and I crumbled to the ground. I lay bunched up, unmoving.

"Let's get outta here. His buddy Zeek'll take care of him." I heard Brazon walk away.

Triton hesitated. Maybe he would stay. Maybe he believed me. Maybe. Then I heard him turn and slowly stride away.

Thus began my real friendship with Zeek.

Chapter 6

I felt a hand supporting my shoulder, urging me up. As my head rolled up along with the rest of me, a warm trickle made its way from my nose down my lips and chin to where it hesitated only long enough to pool into a drop and detach itself. I forced my eyes open to see the red drop splat against the dust and sit for a second until it was absorbed into a circle of red-tainted mud.

My head pounded and my ears rang rhythmically to the throbbing. I swept the bangs out of my eyes and held them back while I pressed my head gingerly with my fingertips, trying to rub away the pain.

The thought suddenly occurred to me that I had never taken such a punch before. Oh, I had been in my share of fights, that was true, but those were always wrestling matches with a few misguided hook shots that only sliced at the air. The closest I had come to hitting my target was when my fist connected with Tommy Brawshaw's ear. That sent him yelping home to his mother and put me in the doghouse for a week. But never had the opponent's fist found its mark on me. Brazon just had to be the first.

Then the realization of what I had just done came screaming at me full-force. Not only had I just openly befriended the class reject, which undoubtedly would throw me into the same category, I also just ruined my friendship with my two best buddies. No, I hadn't just ruined those friendships; I had very successfully created a new target for them. And I knew better than anyone what kind of torment that would result in. I let my head drop into my hands and ignored the blood as it ran freely from my nose to the ground.

Why? Why had I been so stupid? I should have just left the whole thing alone. I could've tried talking to them again. Triton would've eventually listened. He might've understood.

No! I told myself sarcastically. *I couldn't have done that. I had to go barreling into the whole mess full steam.* I squeezed my eyes shut tightly at the memory.

It won't be easy, but it will be right. I almost looked around to see who had spoken, but then I knew. I paused a moment, hoping for more. No more words, but a sense of calm consumed me. Ok. So now what?

As if answering my thoughts, Zeek's voice broke the silence. "You'll be sore awhile." I knew it was him, yet he sounded different, something in his voice had changed. He sounded older, wiser maybe.

I felt the support again of his two scrawny hands as they slid under my arms from behind and pulled me fully to my feet. I was surprised at his strength. He let me regain my dignity for a moment before he nudged me on the shoulder.

"C'mon. Let's go." There was something almost commanding about his tone and even about the way he acted and carried himself. It seemed so odd that I forced myself to look him straight in the eye. What I saw there in his face was a complete transformation from the stooge who had been the butt of the cruel slapstick jokes. He was, well, in charge. He almost reminded me of an older brother who is around to pick up his kid brother after his first real fight. I had been picked up, dusted off, and was now ready to be taken home.

He seemed to fit his new character perfectly during the silent walk home. I'd wipe the blood from my nose with the tag end of my T-shirt, and he'd pretend not to notice. I brushed the dirt from my arms and straightened my hair by running a hand back where the part should have been, but he never broke his slow, steady stride.

And when we reached my corner, he paused for a moment as if debating whether to finish the walk to my house. He darted forward suddenly, quickened his pace, and blurted out nervously, “Why’d you do it?”

I couldn’t think fast enough. I wasn’t sure if I should tell him that I knew about everything or if I should apologize for my lame attempts at being his friend or if I should just play the whole thing off. I shrugged.

A hint of the old Zeek snuck up as he shot me a side-glance. “Thanks,” he said sheepishly, then turned on his heel and strode down the street.

There it was. That was the reason. Zeek. I did it for Zeek. I had finally done what was right, and it even seemed at the moment as if the whole mess was worth it. And yet, I had no idea of what was to come.

The screen door announced my entrance as it banged shut noisily behind me. I held a wad of T-shirt to my nose, knowing better than to drip blood across Mom’s new hardwood floor. Once in the bathroom, I stripped off my shirt, which by now was covered with a large, bright red stain. I leaned over the basin and splashed ice-cold water on my face in an effort to wash away enough blood to get a good look at the damage.

What I was hit with was a sad reflection of my fighting ability. The bloated midsection of my nose seemed to be growing larger by the second. It flattened and distorted the way my nose looked, reminding me of a boxer in the ninth round.

I stepped around the corner, trying to keep my head tilted back and the blood from dripping while I searched the freezer for an ice bag. I knew Mom always kept a few ready. I felt the edge of one in the back corner and was trying to carefully extract it and avoid an avalanche of frozen meat, vegetables, popsicles, and ice cream. I had nearly completed my mission when a voice from behind me startled me into a jerk that brought the whole right side of the freezer tumbling to the kitchen floor.

"Mike! Oh my heavens! What on earth happened to you?"

I didn't want to turn around. All she had gotten so far was the side view: torn and bloody T-shirt, scratched and bloody arms, head tilted back awkwardly. I didn't want to see her reaction when she got her first glimpse of the whole picture.

"Honey, turn around here and let me see you." Well, there weren't too many choices at that point. So I stuffed the towel up to the end of my nose and turned around slowly. "Oh!" was all that she could say. She seemed frozen to her spot as her eyes grew larger and larger in a look of disbelief. Nurse Rassonawski had lost her composure. It was so totally unexpected that we stood staring at each other for what seemed to be an endless amount of time.

I finally broke the deadlock. "It's only a bump. It'll be fine."

"No," she was apparently coming out of her trance, "no, it's broken."

Broken?! No, that just couldn't be!

"It's not broken," I said with an assurance that contradicted my real fears.

"I'm sure it is. It looks just awful! Mike, what happened?"

"I just . . ." I swallowed hard, ". . . just got into . . . a little . . . well . . . a little fight."

"A *little* one?? Who on earth with?"

"Nobody important. Don't worry about it."

"Nobody important?" She rolled her eyes. "Nobody important?" She emphasized with increasing volume. Then she drew herself up to full height, sucked in a long breath of air, and gave me a look that told me one indisputable fact. I was about to be lectured.

"Mike Rassonawski." *Yep. Here we go.* She searched through the frozen landfill at my feet and retrieved a Scooby Doo ice pack. She thrust it at me as she continued. "I don't at all like the way you have been acting lately. What has gotten into you? Coming home with your nose smashed in?" Involuntarily, I lifted a hand to my nose, now covered in Scooby iciness. "Arguing with your best friends? I've seen a very noticeable change in you, and I don't like it one bit, young man. Now I want to know who you were fighting with."

I felt a trap. Either I come clean, or I was in big trouble.

"Our football game just got a little rough." Well, that was true.

"Who?" It was a command. No wiggle-room.

"Brazon."

"One of your closest friends? I should've known. With the way you've been acting lately, I should have expected that. What exactly happened?"

Now I was in a real spot. If I told her that I had gotten into it with Brazon over Zeek, who she had warned me to stay away from, I'd be in real trouble. If I lied and got caught, I'd be in worse trouble. And from her look, I wasn't going to get by without some kind of explanation.

"Ugh . . . " I started slowly, ". . . well, he ticked me off because he was picking on some littler kid." *That's close to the truth.* "And when I told him to knock it off, he got all mad and started pushing. One thing just let to another, and here I am."

"That's it? That's the whole story?" She obviously didn't believe me. But I decided to stick to my explanation.

"Yep. That's it."

"And where does the Zeekman boy fit in?"

Zeek? How did she know about him? I knew I needed to tread lightly here. I could see her dangling a carrot as she led me to the noose.

"Zeek?" I acted surprised. "Why do you think he had anything to do with it?"

"Oh," now she was letting me sweat, "you just happened to run into him on the walk home?"

"Actually, yeah, I did just *happen* to run into him today. So what?" At least now I knew that she had just seen him walking home with me.

"So what?" She shook her head and pointed her finger at me to emphasize. "Don't you get smart with me! You were told to stay away from that Zeekman boy - he's nothing but trouble." I nearly grinned at the irony of that statement, but caught myself. "I don't want you anywhere near him!"

"Why do you have it in for Zeek? What's he ever done to you?" I said smartly, forgetting her warning.

"Oh, I think you know. Maybe you know a lot more than I thought you did." She looked at me suspiciously. Then she raised her eyebrows, softening. "Mike, I brought you up knowing right from wrong. Don't get mixed up in anything that you know is wrong."

"What happened to helping out people who need it? Isn't that what you and Dad preach? Actually, isn't that what they preach at church?"

She narrowed her eyes and tilted her head as her stare burned a hole in me. "So, you are going to play that angle?" My genuine look of confusion must have been taken for a sarcastic one. "Confused?" she continued pointedly. "Well, maybe two week's grounding might help you sort things out."

Two weeks? For getting into a fight? I had sure picked the wrong day to get her riled up.

I started to say something, but gratefully, was interrupted. "But for now, let's get you to the doctor."

Things seemed to be going from bad to worse. Dr. Rein confirmed Mom's suspicions and made his diagnosis apparent with two wide strips of white tape strapped across my nose, and worse yet, wads of cotton packing stuffed inside. Nice. He sent me home with painkillers and a warning that two black eyes would be visible by morning. Real nice.

So, I was grounded for two weeks with so much gauze stuffed up my nose that I couldn't even breathe. Lying on my bed and tossing the football in the air, I was wondering what kind of mess I had gotten myself into and why doing something right seemed so incredibly difficult.

God, I've made a real mess of things. I tried doing it my way and we both know it didn't work so well. I didn't think it through. I sure didn't wait on You. Help me. I'm ready to listen and follow Your plan.

I was reminded immediately of the story our youth pastor had used to illustrate a point just a few weeks ago. Some guy had gone to a fancy restaurant with his friends, and as he was engrossed in his conversation he accidentally knocked over his hot tea. When it hit the white wall, it left a terrible stain. The owner was furious, said the stain would never come out, and threatened to make the guy pay for it to be repainted. Everyone was surprised when a stranger at a nearby table offered to correct the problem. He left the restaurant and returned with an artist's set of paintbrushes and a pallet of paint. He sat down and began creating a scene from the brown stain. As they watched, it became a beautiful mural of wildlife. Then the artist signed his name, and everyone was shocked because he was some famous painter. He turned the mess into a masterpiece. Our youth pastor described how God could do that for us when we make mistakes. *Well, this is sure one of those times. I've made an absolute mess of things. Would You turn it into a masterpiece, even though I can't imagine how?*

I smiled inwardly, happy to relinquish control of the situation to the One who was the true Artist. A sense of peace filled me and for the first time in a long time, I had a feeling that everything would actually work out. *It may not be easy.* The thought seemed to come from nowhere, and yet I knew exactly where it did come from. *Ok Lord. It won't be easy, but if it's Your plan, it will be right. Help me when it gets hard? Cuz I have a feeling it's going to.*

I heard the back door. Dad. He was home from his golf game. I knew what was going to happen next. It was policy in our family that if I got in trouble with Mom and things weren't worked out by the time Dad got home, he would straighten things out.

I heard him wrestle around with the twins some, and then sit down at the table. After the normal chit-chat, their voices got hushed and I knew my story was being replayed.

"Boys, go to your playroom. Your mom and I need to talk." Uh-oh. Things weren't sounding good. Then I heard footsteps and figured I was next.

"Mike?"

"Yeah?"

"Can I come in?" He was asking? Maybe things weren't so bad.

"Sure, Dad. Door's open."

As he came in I instantly tried to read his face. I was surprised by his expression. It wasn't anger, or the sternness that I had expected. It looked more like concern, or maybe even worry. He sat on the edge of my bed and stole the ball from me mid-air.

"Broken, huh? That's going to be sore for a few days."

"Yeah."

"Probably get a couple of shiners out of it too."

"Nice."

"Much pain now?"

"Nah."

With the small talk out of the way, Dad paused and looked around the room uncomfortably.

"I've been talking to your mom. She thinks maybe something's going on with you." Then he looked me straight in the eye. "Are you in any trouble, Mike?" He seemed to study me, looking for something in my face, or my eyes.

"No. I'm not in any trouble. except with Mom, that is. And I'm not really sure why."

"She says you've been fighting with your friends,"

"Yeah," I agreed.

"She just doesn't understand that a fight or two can be normal for us guys, right?"

"Yeah, sure." The way he said "normal" made me wonder what he was really getting at.

"But what about that Zeekman kid?"

Oh no! Not him too?

In a pinched voice that sounds like it came from someone else, I asked, "Yeah, what about him?" I tried coming off nonchalant, hoping that my lack of interest might draw out some answers.

"Your mom and I don't want you near him, Mike. And we mean it." He paused and looked at me thoughtfully. "Now you know that we've never tried to choose your friends for you, but this is one time we have to step in."

"Why? Dad, what is wrong with Zeek?" I posed defensively.

"Let me ask you this: why all of a sudden, have you started hanging around him?"

"I haven't really, Dad. I'm just trying to be nice to the guy. He just . . . has a lot of problems, that's all."

Suddenly Dad's attitude changed. He seemed strangely subdued. "You're right; he does. That's exactly why we don't want you anywhere near him. I feel sorry for the kid, but I won't sacrifice your future. That's the end of this discussion."

The end? Oh no, I knew better than that. The way things were going, I was sure that it was only the beginning.

Chapter 7

I protested. It wasn't right. I knew somewhere there was a rule about it. When a guy broke his nose, he didn't have to go to school the next day. I was certain, but it didn't matter. My objections were wasted. The doctor didn't have to set my nose and the best I got was a painkiller and decongestant.

As I drug myself slowly down the block, I foolishly allowed my mind to linger on the possibilities that the day held: jeers from the back of math class, my lunch plate "accidentally" overturned, and the bathroom door held shut, books dumped out of my locker - all of our best pranks for Zeek. I was sure there would be a new recipient today.

I purposely chose a new route to my bus pick-up point, knowing that Brazon, Triton, and I always teamed up on the regular path. Still, once I reached the corner where the bus would meet us, I realized that I would have to face the inevitable. Maybe that's why I drug my feet as if walking the final mile to death row. Maybe. Or more likely, I was hoping deep down that I would miss the bus.

That's when I saw him. His outline emerged slowly from the alley up ahead and as he rounded the corner on his way to the same destination, my fears grew. It felt as if a burning hot coal sat at the bottom of my gut. Just seeing him brought back all the events from the day before.

I watched as he moved timidly down the street. Shoulders slumped, hands shoved in his pockets, eyes warily scanning his path. He jerked his head in an effort to flip back his bangs and moved forward in slow, measured strides.

I realized with sudden regret that I was getting just a taste of what he endured every day: the dread of torment dished out by classmates that valued a laugh more than a person's feelings, and the animal instinct to hide rather than endure the pain. And suddenly, ferociously, the weight of guilt nearly buckled my knees: *I* was the one who had caused such anguish, and without a second thought. Until now.

My mind short-circuited from the overload of thoughts and fears. What should I do next? Maybe I should call to Zeek. We could face the onslaught together. Maybe I should wait, and then jump on the bus at the last minute. Maybe I should just walk up and pretend that nothing had happened. But with a cross-eyed look down at my bandaged nose, I knew that wasn't going to fly. Maybe I should just . . . die. How could I have gotten myself into such a mess?

Though I was nearly a block behind him, Zeek suddenly turned on his heel, startled. Seeing me, he relaxed and I noticed again that eager, tail-wagging look. But he was still unsure of my intentions, no doubt due to my earlier betrayal. So he waited, remaining still.

A nod was all I could muster. That was enough. I was as good as a *'Come on over here, boy!'* Zeek was dashing forward as if in a race. He was at my side before I took another step.

He gave me a quick side-glance. "How are you doing?" A hint of that brotherly tone snuck through his question.

"Alright. I guess."

"Is it broken?"

"Yep."

We walked for a few steps in an uncomfortable silence.

"Let's hang back here," I suggested nervously.

Eager to please, he agreed. So we stopped and stood. For some reason, I felt pressed to make conversation. Zeek seemed perfectly happy just standing. Waiting.

"You didn't have any homework?" I noticed he wasn't carrying a book bag or any papers.

"Nope." He grinned awkwardly, and then looked back at the bus pick-up point.

As he looked away, I noticed that for once his clothes seemed to match and he even had on a decent pair of jeans. His long-sleeved shirt was torn slightly at the shoulder, but clean enough. To a perfect stranger, he would appear fairly average. But I wasn't a stranger, and when I happened to glance at his neck in the bright morning light, I could see the large greenish brown areas. These were hidden rather effectively beneath his straggly hair, some close enough to his collar to be shadowed and go unnoticed. I was certain that he was betting the same when he picked this particular shirt to wear.

Despite the fading, those bruises seemed to be screaming for attention. They reminded me that my imagination had only experienced the kind of hell that Zeek actually lived through. They urged me that no matter what my friends, or ex-friends, would say, I would not betray Zeek again. Even as I was thinking it, the yellow blur of our school bus skidded into my line of vision and I knew the test was about to begin.

I tried not to remember every explicit detail of the day as I lay in bed well before my expected bedtime that night. I knew it wouldn't do me any good, that it would only cause me to dread the next day even more, but I couldn't seem to stop myself. It was like an obnoxious tune that played over and over and over in some hidden part of my brain. The more I concentrated on getting rid of it, the louder it became. My memories did the same.

If only Brazon could have been sick, the day might have been tolerable. Triton seemed oddly distant. He just watched the action from a distance, not wanting to be involved. And by the end of the day, he was teaming up with some of the varsity players, ready to get away from the whole mess.

What Triton left undone, Brazon was determined to make up for. We barely caught the bus; we were the last ones on. As usual, everyone was strategically sitting toward the rear, so I immediately grabbed the opportunity to jump in the front seat. Zeek, now the obedient puppy, followed closely.

"Fag section up front!" Brazon announced from his normal seat in the far back corner. So much for great planning. I now realized that every comment would be broadcast loudly over the entire bus so that it would reach our target with plenty of volume and venom. "Hey, Zeeky," he continued. Zeek got an idiotic grin on his face and turned around. I jabbed him in the ribs and whispered, "Ignore him." But Zeek was too used to playing along. "You two aren't holding hands or nothin' up there, are ya?" Laughter broke from the back of the bus, and I lowered myself considerably in the seat.

"No, course not," Zeek grinned.

"No, course not," Brazon mocked in a sing-song girlish voice. Zeek laughed openly.

I poked him again. "Don't let him make a fool of you," I hissed. Zeek look slightly confused, but finally turned around.

The tone had been set for the day. As I sat scrunched low in my seat, I realized that I would need every advantage I could get just to survive this day. My first task was to pull off the white adhesive tape that announced my broken nose, and consequently Brazon's victory, to the world. If Zeek noticed the delicate procedure, he didn't mention it.

There were whispers and muffled voices and a lot of laughter from the back section of the bus. Without even looking, I knew exactly what was going on. We were the butt of all of their imbecile jokes, and when the subdued tones continued for more than a few minutes, I knew they were scheming. How many times had I been a part of that? The tormentor now becoming the tormented. It was the theme that haunted me for the entire day.

Making me suffer through the rest of the bus ride was probably stage I of the plan. It killed me to not be in my regular seat and part of the regular banter, even adding my ingenious details to our schemes. How ironic that I was the brains behind the best of those plots, yet I was soon to discover that I knew nothing of the depth of their deviousness.

Zeek seemed totally unaffected by the whole turn of events. His glassy look was fixed on the window. One strand of his slick, jet-black hair fell across his forehead. He swung it back in place and thoughtlessly gave it a pat to keep it there. *He really is a Geek*, I thought to myself. Although his clothes had definitely improved, he still wore his semi-oily hair in that idiotic 50's style. We were all sure that he didn't have to buy any special creams or gels to keep it back; days without shampoo would do as nicely.

My thoughts were broken when the bus's momentum suddenly reversed. I steadied myself. As the bus driver eased off of his brakes, I could feel the effects of momentum lessen and I relaxed again. But not for long. I was out of my seat and down the bus steps before the driver had the chance to apply final pressure to the brakes and bring the bus to a complete stop.

"Hey, kid. Everybody in their seats until the doors open." His look left me no choice. I turned around and started back to my front row hiding spot.

Satisfied with my obedience, the driver snapped the doors open after I was back in place. As if the starting gates had just been opened in the tenth race, I immediately swung around, ready to burst through. But I wasn't quite fast enough.

I heard the sickening thud before I felt the pain of my fingers being smashed into the iron supporting bar that doubled as a handrail. An instinctive jerk informed me that my flattened fingers weren't about to move.

"In a hurry, Sissy-nowski?" I didn't need to look up at the source of the mocking voice. There was no time to wonder at how Brazon made it to the front of the bus so swiftly, obviously part of his plan. "How's the nose? It looks painful. But I think that will be the least of your worries today." Brazon's tone drilled into my brain.

I concentrated on how to knock off the book that was pinning my hand and causing the throbbing pain working its way up my arm. But he was leaning his full weight onto it, and I had no leverage from a step down.

"Let's get moving!" the driver commanded, oblivious to the confrontation.

"Just wait," Brazon hissed. "We'll see what kinda tough guy you really are." As he spat the final word, he unexpectedly lifted the vice and released my hold. I went tumbling out the door with a few cartoon-style steps. After regaining my balance, I rushed toward the school with no thought other than getting away from Brazon. I ventured a quick glance around and was surprised to see Zeek glued to my side.

I paused in front of the school doors, debating my options. I wanted to turn and see where Brazon and Triton were, but I wouldn't allow myself. How to get to my first hour class? I could charge right in and head straight to the math room since I happened to have my books with me from my homework over the weekend. Then I would sit in an empty classroom like an idiot with my new-found friend for ten whole minutes before the first bell rang. No thanks.

I could hang outside for ten minutes until I heard the bell ring, then dash to the math room, hoping not to run into Brazon and Triton. Little chance of that; they always waited until the last minute too.

I could try to act casual, just head for my locker like normal, shoot the breeze awhile, and then head for class. Yeah right, that would allow plenty of time for the humiliation to continue. I almost laughed at how ridiculous it was to plan how to get to my first class. I had sunk to a new all-time low.

I looked over at Zeek for some possible help. He was staring at me with his stupid clown-grin plastered on his face. It was one of those what-are-we-going-to-do-now looks. *Fat lotta help he's going to be. Geez, out of all people, I'd think he would have figured out some way of avoiding the torment. He had to face it every day.*

I wasn't about to get used to their treatment. Triton's locker was three or four down to the left of mine, but Brazon's was just one over to the right. I glanced around quickly, trying to make a notation of everyone else's positions and strategies. Zeek was suddenly nowhere to be seen. He must have slid around the corner quietly to his locker. Triton was busy digging in his locker, obviously undaunted by my appearance. With my locker door open, I couldn't see anything down Brazon's way. But I knew he was there.

I dug around aimlessly in my locker for what seemed hours, and then decided it was close enough to class time. As I reached for my pencil, I heard a familiar voice speaking softly, and then laughing openly. Without thinking, I immediately swung my locker door shut in hopes of catching a glimpse of Maria. I didn't need to rush. She seemed to be posing for the picture that would become burned into my mind.

She was facing Brazon as he leaned easily against the lockers. He reached out and slid his arm around her waist and drew her closer to him. He whispered something to her and she let her hand glide down his arm. They both laughed and turned towards me.

"Maria says she loves your new look," he taunted. "She says that fat nose covers up more of your ugly mug, and that's a definite improvement."

She slapped his arm, pretending to be offended, but allowed him to whisper something more into her ear.

I slammed my locker shut and stormed to the stairway. What was she thinking? Why would she even let him touch her? Surely she could see through his flirting and tell what kind of guy he was, couldn't she? Well, it wasn't my problem. I wasn't going to care. I had plenty of other things to worry about, like surviving the rest of the day.

As I rounded the first flight of stairs, suddenly eager for the solitude of an empty classroom, I found myself in a new predicament. Waiting at the top platform was Triton. He was all alone. His back was towards me as he leaned against the wall. His fists were jammed into his pockets, and I could see a row of bulging knuckles through the denim.

He was waiting. For me, no doubt. And I knew he heard me as I pounded up the stairs, so there was no retreating. But why wasn't he acknowledging me? I stood frozen, unsure of my next move. Would he single-handedly pin me to the wall and hold me there by the neck while my feet dangled in an effort to touch the ground? A quick glance around the staircase and hallways proved that no teachers were on guard to break up a fight.

Realizing my options were limited, I started up the remaining four stairs slowly, yet with determination. As I reached Triton, I side-stepped around him carefully. He didn't move.

"I'm not gonna try to figure out what's going on," he mumbled, almost to himself. "I sure don't get this deal with Zeek," he continued, "but I'll tell ya, Brazon's got it out for you. Watch yourself."

"Yea, I will," I answered, hoping that was the end of his message. "Thanks."

He turned and strode away.

Triton was confused, but at least he hadn't completely sided with Brazon. Maybe things weren't as bad as I had expected.

I allowed myself to wander into the empty math room and pause momentarily before I chose a neutral middle row seat. I flipped through my book absently, trying to kill time.

"There you are. I was wondering where you went." Zeek. The same greasy strand of hair had fallen across his forehead. "Got here early, huh?"

"Uh-huh."

"Mind if I sit?" he said as he slipped into the desk next to mine.

This was just great. There we were, the two of us, outcasts, sitting alone in a silence that seemed to mock us. This was definitely not the plan that I would have concocted. I knew what it would look like to the first few who entered the room when the bell rang. I was praying that would not be Brazon or Triton.

The suddenness of the bell shattered the silence. In the distance, I could hear lockers slamming, books slapping together, and voices and footsteps getting louder and louder as they advanced to their first hour classes.

Our math teacher was fortunately the first one through the doors. She gave us an odd look, then proceeded to her desk as she casually mentioned, "Well, you're here early boys. Eager for your day of education to begin?" She looked at us almost suspiciously.

The onslaught of students followed. Fortunately, Brazon and Triton were close to the last ones to come in. The seats around us were already filled and they were forced to sit on opposite sides of the room. It seemed a safe enough distance and for the first time that morning, I breathed a sigh of relief.

Math could not have lasted long enough for me that day. As I watched the minute hand move lazily around in circles, I silently willed it to stop. When the bell rang for the next class period, I pretended to work up some last minute calculations when I felt someone behind me.

"Workin' hard?" he breathed hotly in my ear. "Why don't you work on this?" he hissed, then deliberately spat a pile of bubbled saliva onto the center of my paper.

My blood boiled as I stared at the wet spot growing on my paper. That was it. I caught Brazon by surprise as I jumped from my seat and wrapped a death grip around his scrawny neck from behind. He tried to break it several times, then resorted to kicking and twisting to free himself.

"Boys! Enough! I'll have none of your horseplay in my room. Now get out!" Miss Klein demanded from five foot one inch frame. But she meant it, and I wasn't up for a detention. I loosened my grip and Brazon swung around angrily.

"It ain't over," he threatened.

I walked out of the room and went straight to biology. I began to breathe easier when I mentally mapped out the rest of my morning: I was taking advanced science while Brazon and Triton were barely squeaking through earth science. Then I had Spanish while they were stuck in remedial English. And the last hour before lunch, I was busy beating on the drums while Triton lifted weights and Brazon had study hall.

The morning did pass easily. Of course, there was a bombardment of questions about my nose. Apparently removing the tape did little to deter attention from the swelling and the purple-blackness creeping below both eyes. I tried to play it off casually, but word had gotten around that Brazon had "beat me up."

Lunch began an angry turn of events. I had always been thankful for the strategic positioning of our band room, which just happened to be next to the cafeteria. Since I didn't have a complicated instrument to tear apart, I was always the first to the door and in line for lunch.

I usually saved several places for Brazon, Triton, and a couple of other lucky friends. Suddenly I lost my appetite as I realized that I would probably be sitting alone through lunch. Zeek was one of the few students who actually volunteered as a kitchen aid. The first day of school he signed on. Maybe he did have his ways of avoiding us. Right then, I wished that the kitchen staff needed more help.

I had just set my milk carton back into the center section of my lunch tray. I reached toward the center of the table, grabbing for the salt, when I heard the crunch and felt the cold liquid splash all over my arm and shirt. His fist was still smashed pointedly into my carton as he grabbed my shirt collar.

"This is gonna be you by the end of the day," he sneered at the flattened carton and the milk that seeped over the rest of my lunch.

"Sure," I countered as I broke his grip and marched defiantly out of the cafeteria.

Once I found the reprieve of the abandoned hallways, I was at a loss. What was I going to do for the rest of the day? What was I going to do for the next fifteen minutes? I knew there had to be school staff patrolling the hallways, just looking for deviants and troublemakers on the loose. I wouldn't be allowed to wander at will, skirting encounters with Brazon.

Hide. My first and strongest instinct was to hide. The whole afternoon? I realized that would be impossible, but at least between classes. That was the time I would be openly hunted. And now. Yes, definitely now.

This new consolidated school was not designed with a lot of secret passageways or rooms, but I racked my brain for the perfect spot nonetheless. The janitor's room, maybe? No. They were in and out so much I knew I'd be caught. The classrooms? No, they were all locked over the noon hour. The locker room? Maybe. But Coach would return before class and I'd have to deal with him. Where then? I could feel the panic as it tightened around my neck, forcing me to take shorter and quicker breaths of air. I could hear lunch trays being stacked and knew that soon the halls would be busy until the sixth hour bell. The bathroom was my only choice.

I raced in and found the last stall open for me to take cover. After locking the door, I stood for a moment, debating. I could act like I was actually using the john, but that would limit the amount of time I could hide there. Or . . . I carefully stepped up on the toilet seat and squatted there, trying to find a comfortable position leaning against the tank. If the door was locked with no feet visible, everyone would probably think the toilet was broken and just leave it at that - I hoped.

I kept a careful eye on my watch. Twelve minutes until the sixth hour bell. Then three more minutes to get to class. I'd escape with a minute and a half to spare. That'd be just enough time to get my books for the rest of the afternoon and make sixth hour study hall, if I ran.

The bathroom wasn't a busy place during the lunch hour. Teachers on hall patrol were pretty careful about not letting a gang in the boys' bathroom at the same time. One or two guys wandered in, did their business, and left. A couple guys hung out a little longer, probably just killing time. My door was only tried once, and then left without a second thought.

Five minutes until the bell. The room was empty. Brazon must've gone outside or to the gym to waste lunch hour. Suddenly I felt tremendously foolish. Why was I running from him anyway? Because of his threats? No. I knew I could hold my own with him. Because he had rounded up a new set of groupies who would follow his every command? Maybe. But most likely, it was because of the way he treated me - laughed at me and talked me down, like . . .well, like he did Zeek. And that was what had me crouched on the toilet seat for the entire lunch hour.

Yet from some buried corner inside of me, a bit of pride began to surface. It stirred my growing feeling of resentment and indignation. What was I doing hiding and cowering? I needed to stand up for myself and not let Brazon or anyone else walk all over me.

My knees ached from my awkward position on the stool, and I felt a pang of relief as I straightened them and forced them to carry my weight. The sliding lock clicked ominously in the silent room. As I walked out of the stall, I was met with my own reflection. The pale, frightened look of fear was apparent even beneath the bruised eyes and puffy nose. I sucked in a full breath of air and told myself there was nothing to be afraid of. Boy, was I wrong.

I had turned and was moving toward the door, gaining confidence with each step. Just as I reached for the handle, the door moved. I backed up a step, a frozen statue watching the scene.

The door burst open and Zeek came flying in at me, colliding with my midsection. I recovered easily, but Zeek landed squarely on the floor, face down. I grabbed him by the arm and helped him back to his feet. Suddenly aware that I had an audience, I turned back defensively.

"Awwww . . . ain't that swwwweeet?" mocked Brazon, his arms now crossed with his shoulder leaning to one side. "Why don't you kiss it and make it feel all better?" he continued.

"Why don't you get outta my face?" I snarled back. He didn't scare me, and maybe if I showed that, the three guys behind him would back off too.

I wondered briefly who they were. I had seen a couple of them and realized they were from Sparta, but why were they so quick to side with Brazon? Did they know each other? Maybe they just enjoyed a good taunting like everyone else.

"I ain't been in your ugly face yet." Brazon came at me suddenly with all of his new buddies at his heels. He had me pinned against the wall with his forearm before I had time to react. Out of the corner of my eye, I caught Zeek as he tried to run interference for me. One of Brazon's goons had him flattened before he even got close.

My mind was racing in circles, trying to figure a way out of this mess, when Brazon drew up close to my face and scowled, "You did a stupid thing yesterday, really stupid." A fist in my air sack marked the end of his warning. The force of it doubled me over. I felt myself drop to the floor as I lay sucking air.

Then distinct footsteps and a gruff voice. "What's going on here?"

Brazon and the others were silent as they were escorted roughly out of the room. Then apparently, the voice was directed towards us, however, the pain and humiliation created a fog that made it difficult to focus. "You boys get to the nurse." Recognition dawned slowly as our principal continued, "Then report to my office."

Fortunately, that had been the worst of it for the day. Zeek and I reported to the nurse, who checked us over thoroughly, and announced that she believed my nose had been broken. News flash. I produced my doctor's excuse from PE, and she released us with warnings of soreness and aching muscles. Mr. Scott, our principal, drilled us with the routine questions for awhile, then sent us to our seventh hour class with the assurance that we wouldn't need to worry about an incident like that happening again. No detentions, no lectures, no sixth hour class. Actually, we made out fairly well on the whole.

We came in on the middle of seventh hour PE. I waited with Zeek as he got dressed, finding myself feeling more and more comfortable with him. Still, it seemed odd to be jokingly discussing whether or not Nurse Thomas would be interested in dating younger men as we walked to the football field. It was actually easy to talk to Zeek. I didn't have to work at being funny or clever, I could just be myself. He didn't seem to expect anything more.

When we reached the field, Zeek handed Coach his pass and raced out onto the field to join the improvised game of field hockey. I hung back for a break in the action so I could talk to Coach and give him the doctor's excuse.

Coach Milan was intense with all sports, even practice in PE, and we had all learned early not to disturb him while he was concentrating. However, he was also the most popular coach with the kids. They all claimed he was a great guy, so I hoped he would prove true to his reputation when I showed him my release form. He blew the whistle and ran onto the field to make a call and start the play over. I wondered to myself whether or not he even knew I was there. But when he ran back to the sideline, he shoved the clipboard at me.

"Here, Mike. You can keep track of the score," he said easily enough.

He had not asked for my pass, or checked the time on it. Somehow I knew he hadn't forgotten. He trusted me and was showing that. I quickly jammed the pink slip of paper in my pocket, feeling boosted for the first time that day.

"I heard what happened," he started out of nowhere, not even looking at me. Wow, the teachers' network worked fast. "I don't know what caused it, but I do know Zeekman needs a friend." He was watching the game intently, trying to lead this discussion very nonchalantly. I wasn't sure if he expected a response. I said nothing.

"C'mon Blue!" he suddenly shouted. "You've got to swing over and cover that gap!" Then back to me, "Did you get that point?"

"Uh-huh."

"And I've heard about the Brazon kid. Don't let him get to ya. You're too good a kid to be hanging around with him anyways." What? That was a turnaround. Wondering what he meant by that, I almost missed his final comment. "Hey, I still want you to show up for practice tonight." That was all he said.

But it was enough. It was enough to convince me that what I had done was right. I thanked God quickly for the show of support. I would need all I could get in the upcoming weeks.

Chapter 8

The following days were a blur of threats, ultimatums, strategic avoidance plans. But somehow, by the end of the second week, the fuse which had ignited Brazon's temper seemed to have been dampened. When the dismissal bell rang Friday afternoon, after only one minor incident between classes, he passed by me without so much as a snide remark. It was as if I weren't even there. As if he had more important things on his mind.

He and Maria were obviously still together, but I had seen her head for the bus a few minutes earlier. So she wasn't the cause of his distraction.

My curiosity got the best of me, and I found myself lingering behind him just far enough to be out of sight, but close enough to see what was distracting him. He burst out of the doors in a dead run and I stood frozen at the end of the hallway watching, bewildered. At first I thought he was headed towards our bus, but after another minute, I saw him flag down an old beat-up car and jump in the back. I didn't recognize the car or anyone in it. The whole incident left me with a very uneasy feeling.

There was no football practice Friday night due to the Varsity game, so I made my way out to our bus. I looked forward to the break I got on Fridays, especially now that I had become the team's errand runner during practices. I didn't really care though, since Brazon was kicked off the team the day of our "incident" in the bathroom. Coach wanted me to stay up on all the plays, just in case I got the doctor's approval to play before the end of the season.

Triton and I had spoken a few times only briefly, but long enough to convince me that he was continuing to be a neutral bystander in this whole ordeal. For the most part, he had just buried himself in football and stayed away from all of us. News was out that Triton was on the Varsity starting line-up for the first time that night. I couldn't wait to watch him.

As the bus jerked to a stop at Milton Central pick-up point, Zeek and I finalized our plans to meet at the football field for the game. I was still being cautious of Mom and her recent obsession with Zeek. A little planning ahead of time would prevent a major confrontation with her. The last thing I needed was Mom in my face.

I flipped on the TV and flopped on my usual corner of our worn couch.

"What? You're going to spend some time out of your room today? What's the occasion?" She stood with her hands on her hips filling the doorway so that only thin beams of light could sneak by her.

It was true. I had avoided all conversation and confrontation by spending my free time safely alone in my room. But even then, she found something to harp on. I wasn't acting like myself lately. She didn't like this change in my behavior. That was one of the warning signs: a drastic change in behavior, and she didn't like it, not one little bit. Maybe we'd go and see Dr. Rein and just have this little matter checked.

"No occasion, Mom. Just killin' time." I kept my eyes fixed on the TV.

"I'd think you'd want to be with your friends."

"Nope." I wasn't going to give her the satisfaction of drawing me into her camouflaged interrogation.

"You're planning on going to the game tonight, aren't you?"

"Yup."

"Well good." She sounded relieved.

Zeek and I chose to meet by the south goal post. I left Mom and Dad at their customary front row seats in the parents' section. Then I drifted by the cheering section and made my way slowly back down the ramp at the opposite end of the bleachers. I turned and for a moment allowed myself to watch Maria as she joined the cheerleaders in a thunderous chant. Her long black hair was tied back in a thick braid with bright red bow holding it at the bottom. It swung back and forth rhythmically as she moved side to side with the beat.

As the chant wound down and the other cheerleaders turned to watch the game, I noticed Maria scanning the cheering section, obviously looking for someone. I moved a step closer to the railing, hoping to catch her eye for a moment, letting myself dream that it might be me she was looking for. But then memories of the previous weeks came rushing back. I turned quickly and disappeared before she did see me.

Zeek was already at our meeting point leaning against the thick cable wire that served as a blockade to keep the fans a safe distance from the game. He was all alone, except for a couple of grade schoolers who were playing hide-and-seek far from their parents. The rest of the crowd was following the game at the other end of the field.

Our Mustangs had run a successful series of plays and were now within scoring distance. I wanted to run to the other end and catch the action, but I was still leery of Mom. I didn't know what kind of scene she would cause if she saw me hanging out with Zeek. So I stayed put.

"Pete had a pretty good run,"

"Oh yea. It was real good," he joined in enthusiastically.

"Let's hope we can convert and get some points on the board early," I added.

"Yea, that'd be good."

"Hey," Zeek began hesitantly. "You seen Brazon tonight?" He looked around in a distracted way.

"No." I glanced at him. "Why?"

"Uh, nothing," he lied.

"Really, why do you ask?" I pushed.

"I, uh, just thought I saw him with . . .well, with . . . it doesn't matter."

Now he had my full attention. "What's up?"

"Well, I just thought I saw him, but it probably wasn't." Then he deliberately changed the subject. "He's really left you alone since he met with Mr. Scott, huh?"

"Yea, I wonder why . . ." My train of thought was broken by a boom of cheering from the Sparton fans. Touchdown! Then the hush followed by another burst of screaming, clapping, and horn honking. Yes! Extra points. What a way to start the game!

I had intended to not let the conversation about Brazon drop, but in the excitement of scoring, it was forgotten. We had taken a decisive early lead. But more than that, I knew after the kick, Triton would be playing, and I didn't want to miss a minute of it.

As it happened, Zeek and I had perfect field position to watch Triton in action. His large frame was easy to pick out of the red and white defense line.

The first few plays were safe and boring. It was third and eight, and a pass was inevitable. The whistle blew and the play began. Their offensive line kept our defense at a standstill until . . . out of the middle of the line of locked players one link broke loose. A large blur swallowed the thin frame of the quarterback wearing orange.

"Triton!" I could barely hear myself think above the roar of the crowd. Triton's single-mindedness had left their quarterback still face down while the rest of our defense pounded and jumped on the huddle around their rookie sensation.

"Way to hit, buddy!" I screamed with all I had. My excitement was crushed when a familiar voice cut through the background cheering.

"Buddy?" Cutting laughter and Brazon's snide tone. "Do you think Triton's still your buddy?" The voice was coming from a distance behind me. I battled with whether or not to give him the satisfaction of turning to pinpoint his whereabouts.

I gave in to my instincts and swung around. Brazon was outside of the grounds, leaning against the chain-link fence that separated the field from the adjoining parking lot. It was dark, and I couldn't make out who else was there.

"There isn't anyone I see that's a buddy of you or your freak friend." A mumbled comment was added from behind him which received a roar of approval.

"Whaddya wastin' your time here for?" came clearly from an outline walking away.

"Yea ... you're right," Brazon conceded easily. "There's only one good reason for being around a Zeekman and it ain't here and it ain't now." He turned and walked into the darkness.

"Jerk," I said as I watched them move away. "Who was he was with?"

Zeek turned away with a look that made it obvious he knew the answer, but he shrugged off the question.

"Hey," I swung him around by the crook of his arm. "Don't play it off. Who are they?"

Zeek didn't seem the type to lie easily, and as he nervously kicked his foot into the ground. I could tell he was debating about whether to attempt it or not.

I made it easy for him. "And don't try lying. You're no good at it, so you might as well tell me the truth."

I saw the look of a reluctant decision as he drew a long and heavy sigh. Then he looked me straight in the eye and I knew that I was going to get the answer this time.

"It . . . it was . . . Ted Jansen and a bunch of other guys."

"What? No. It couldn't been. What would Brazon be doing with them?"

Zeek just shrugged as he turned back to the game.

Ted Jansen. It hadn't taken long at our new consolidated school to hear about a few infamous students from Sparta. Jansen was one of them. Everyone knew he was the "get high" connection. Though he usually only dealt with marijuana, everyone knew he was capable of getting and doing more. Much more.

No one would guess his favorite entertainment by just looking at him or talking to him. He came from a popular family - his dad owned the local newspaper and his mom, of all things, was a nurse. Ted was even fairly popular. Though he was a sophomore, he was friendly enough to almost everybody, especially to the junior high students.

"Brazon?" I said slowly as the connection finally sparked. *What is Brazon doing with that guy? I guess that doesn't take too much imagination. But why? Had he changed that much and I just missed it? Or had he been like that all along, and I'm just a dope that didn't know?*

I glanced up to Zeek, searching for answers. His expression left me both startled and puzzled. He was watching me patiently. Watching me put the pieces together, as if he knew all along how things fit.

Yet there was something more. An underlying feeling of fear, maybe even panic that I sensed. It was nothing I could put my finger on. As a matter of fact, he seemed to be working hard to appear normal, calm. But I noticed his breathing had quickened. He rhythmically rubbed his hand on his pant leg, slow and hard, as if dreading the next few moments.

He must have mistaken my silence for accusation or condemnation because he suddenly burst out with an exclamation that nearly made me jump. “Alright! I’ll tell you the whole thing. But you have to listen to it all.” He looked at me wearily. “All of it,” he repeated. “Then you can . . . do whatever.” His tone softened and turned sad. “Whatever you want to do,” he trailed off quietly.

All I could do was nod and try to keep my look as even as possible.

“It’s not me; it’s my dad.” He tiptoed into the explanation. “It’s been going on for awhile now.”

I wondered why he had chosen this moment to explain about his dad. I listened with rapt attention, even with the intermittent cheering in the background. The game seemed suddenly miles away.

“My dad may not be what you think he is.” His words came out slowly, each carefully before measured before they escaped.

It seemed to be so hard for him to tell me. I debated about whether or not to just admit I knew - admit that I was there and had seen, or rather, heard everything. But something wouldn’t let me. Something told me to just listen and not interrupt.

“You see,” he went on, “I know he’s my dad and all, but he does a lot of stuff that’s wrong. Bad. Stuff he shouldn’t. Like . . . drinking too much.” That seemed to be the easy one to admit. “And . . . well, other stuff.

“He’s gotta raise me himself, you know? At first when Mom left, he wouldn’t let me go with her. I thought maybe he wanted me around. Maybe he really cared. Mom must have thought that too, otherwise, she would have taken me, right?” His sudden question surprised me, but I quickly nodded reassurance and he continued.

"Well, he says it's because raising a kid is so hard, and he hates his job, and he doesn't make much money."

I could feel my eyes trying to squeeze shut, expecting to hear the worst, not quite sure whether I was ready to know the details. I realized that I had to be ready if he was actually going to talk about it.

"That's why he does it."

His statement sounded final, like the end of a story. But that couldn't be it. Did he know that I knew? Maybe he figured that's all of an explanation I needed. Maybe I was supposed to ask. Apparently as I watched him, my eyes asked without my even knowing it.

"You don't know what I'm talking about, do you?"

I thought I did.

"The drugs. That's why my dad sells them. And tries to get me to sell them too," Almost before he finished the sentence he added, "But I won't do it. Really, I don't." His eyes begged me to believe him.

Drugs? What did he mean *drugs*? He switched gears so quickly that I was barely keeping up. I thought we were talking about his getting beat up, not drugs. Suddenly I realized that it fit. It was the final puzzle piece. I was spinning this piece of information, lining it up with what I knew, and suddenly it magically locked into place.

Drugs. Of course. Those men at Zeek's house. They acted like drug dealers. And Zeek's dad was real nervous. That'd be why. And the sack - Zeek was supposed to take it somewhere. Did it have drugs in it? Where was he supposed to go? Why?

But he didn't. He said he didn't, and I believed him. The bruises told me he didn't. The horrid sounds of that night told me he didn't.

Now it made sense. The rumors were right. There were drugs being sold in our little town. By Old Man Zeekman. Maybe that's why Mom was so worried about me getting mixed up with Zeek.

My mind was racing around so fast that it felt like the Tilt-O-Wheel at the summer carnival. I couldn't think straight and more than anything, I needed to think straight.

"Let's take a walk," I turned without waiting for his response.

As I swung around away from the bright lights and loud noises of the game, I was hit with a sudden wall of darkness. We walked to the chain-link fence and I let my hand run along the cold links as we followed it out.

As we retreated from the game, the cold darkness seemed to gather us in. The distant cheering from the game played somewhere in the back of my mind, but I was only aware of the crunching of cold gravel under my feet. I concentrated on the sound, trying to block everything else out. But as suddenly as the cold darkness had slapped me in the face, so did the realization that I was in over my head. Drugs? Now what was I supposed to do?

This had started out as a mission to help a guy whose dad was too rough on him. Now I was one of the few who knew about the drug-dealing? Now what brilliant solution was I going to dig up? I squeezed my eyes shut in a silent plea to God. I confessed that I didn't know what to do. I tried to remind myself of what I had heard at my youth group: nothing takes God by surprise. So I was the only one blind-sided. I reminded myself that I knew the One who had the answers.

The game was suddenly an insignificant glow of lights as I inadvertently glanced back from several blocks away. Although I was not consciously deciding a path, we seemed destined to veer toward Zeek's end of town.

Zeek walked along beside me, keeping the pace, but not breaking the silence. Yet, as we neared the corner that led to his street, he picked up the pace in an obvious attempt to continue on straight. I followed his cue eagerly, not really wanting to encounter his house.

"Is that why your dad hits you?" I blurted out without thinking or weighing his reaction. But even if I had taken the time, his response was not what I would have imagined.

He swung me around hard and grabbed at both of my shoulders, but only caught large fistfuls of coat. Still, he held me firmly in place with a threatening look in his eye.

"How'd you know about that?" he spit at me.

"I . . . I was there," I answered, this time more cautiously.

"When?" He gave me a hard jerk as if to shake the answer from me.

"The night at Johnson's farm." His grip began to relax as he recalled the memory. "I was riding my bike back home . . . and saw, well . . . heard . . . everything."

Silence. It was sinking in. Then he suddenly dropped his arms and turned away. I wasn't going to make the first move again. And he didn't offer any discussion at all. He just started walking again; slowly at first, then more deliberately he quickened his steps.

Just when I thought he was lost in his thoughts, he blurted out, "Who'd ya tell?"

"Nobody," I quickly assured him, though the memory of my explanation to Triton and Brazon was still fresh in my mind. At least, I hadn't told anyone that would believe me.

"Good. My dad'd kill me." He stopped and looked me in the eye with an intensity that burned a hole right through me. "He would, you know."

Chapter 9

The empty warehouse seemed to beckon us from its end of the street. I suddenly wondered how we had gotten so far from the game. I could no longer hear the faint cheering or groans of disapproval from the crowds. Only dead silence. I realized that we had left without a word to anyone. I opened my cell. Low battery warning. I quickly shut it again. We wouldn't be gone long.

I toyed with the idea of mentioning that we should head back, but Zeek seemed so deep in thought. As we rounded the corner of the huge old warehouse, he suddenly stopped walking as if he simply couldn't move another step. He leaned heavily against the rusty metal siding and hung his head.

"So, what do we do now?" I asked cautiously, still unsure of how to approach him.

"Whaddaya mean, 'What do we do?' Do we have any choices?" Zeek carried an air of authority that suddenly made me trust his opinion. "I know we should tell someone . . ." his voice trailed off as he thought through the options. "For a long time I thought I could change things." His eyes were focused on a piece of space off in the distance. A painful look slowly clouded his face as he became lost in his memories. "Then, when I realized I couldn't, I thought I could hide it. But that was before." Something snapped him back to reality and his eyes darted to meet mine, "Before he started selling here and before anyone else knew." His voice quieted.

"Tell? You mean, like the cops?" I felt like an ignorant child asking obvious questions.

Zeek sighed deeply and rubbed his temples deliberately. "I've thought a lot about it. If he gets caught, then maybe I would go live with my mom." An involuntary shudder ran through him.

Zeek seemed so different that night. Calm. Confident. Self-assured. If I had met him for the first time that moment, I would've sworn he was ten years older and someone to look up to. It didn't cross my mind that he really was someone to admire. What he had been through took a great deal of courage.

At the same time, things didn't add up. I wanted to scream at him, *"Then why? Day in and day out? Why do you let them make a fool of you? Why did you let us?"* But I didn't ask because I thought I knew the answer. He needed a friend. He needed to fit in somewhere. And maybe sometimes, a person will do anything to fit in.

My thoughts quickly changed direction and for the first time I took a minute to really wonder about Brazon. The change in him seemed so drastic. Had it been gradual, and I just didn't see it coming? Or did he feel like he had lost his old friends and his old "place" and now needed to belong somewhere else? But not with Ted. Brazon should've known better.

The sound of footsteps broke the stillness of the night and shook me from my thoughts.
Zeek was one step ahead of me. He clasped his large sweaty hand over my mouth in a sudden panicked attempt to keep me quiet. When I forced my head around to face him, I saw his eyes bulging widely with a raw look of fear. He jerked his head to one side, indicating for me to follow him. I nodded, and then used both hands to pry his death grip from my mouth. As we sidled down the side of the warehouse, the footsteps grew louder and faster.

We reached the corner that led to the back of the warehouse. Zeek stopped for a minute before rounding it, obviously considering our options. Then a strange new sound entered the darkness. The beat was as steady and rhythmic as the footsteps, but was much slower and heavier.

Zeek grabbed my arm as I strained out from the wall to distinguish the sound. The fear in his eyes told me that he knew what it was. Without any assistance, I suddenly knew, too. A foreboding chill ran up my spine and I could feel the hairs prickle the back of my neck. I concentrated hard on just taking small breaths of air, but felt as if someone had punched me square in the windpipe.

As I listened to the heavy, measured footsteps, I visualized Old Man Zeekman's thick arms swinging unnaturally at his side and his barrel-shaped chest heaving up and down with each breath. I imagined his smoky beer-breath and rancid body odor. But most of all, I could feel myself tremble with a cold, naked fear of how this night might end.

I was relieved to have my thoughts interrupted when Zeek silently motioned me to follow him further into the darkness. I kept my hand on his shoulder and allowed him to guide me through the thick brush. The back of the warehouse met the connecting property with a mass of overgrown bushes and weeds, leaving only a yard or two of nearly impassable land between them. As we crept low to the ground and made our way through the middle of the thickest growth, I felt somewhat more secure. No one could possibly have seen us in there. I slowly began to breathe easier, feeling safe.

I could tell Zeek was slowing and I figured he was thinking the same. We made our way over a fallen limb, but our progress came to an immediate halt when I slipped and awkwardly wedged my foot in a hole. I nearly flipped Zeek backwards as I tried to regain my balance.

"What's wrong?" he demanded in a whisper.

"My foot. It's stuck."

"Are you hurt?" His tone softened.

"I don't think so, but I can't get it out." There was a heavy limb that had closed in on top of the hole, leaving an odd angled entrance, one that my pointed foot slipped into easily. But once my heel popped through, I was trapped. By wiggling my toes around, I could feel the top and sides of the hole wedged around my foot, and I realized there was no good angle to slide my foot back out.

"Now what?" I asked as I felt Zeek's hands probe around the entrance of the hole and then around the intervening log, until he too understood the problem.

"We gotta move this limb," he whispered with an unfamiliar air of confidence. "You can't help much, but if you can push with your heel, it might give some leverage."

"Yeah, okay. Let's try it."

I could hear him move into position, straddling the limb and getting his best grip under it.

"Ready?" he whispered.

"Now," I signaled.

I concentrated the muscles in the back of my calf and thigh and lifted as much as I could. I heard Zeek grunt with the effort of lifting the log. I felt the pressure very slowly being lifted and tried to twist my foot loose. Zeek had the log lifted just inches off of the ground. I felt my foot give slightly and took that as my cue to pull with all I had.

The sudden force must have thrown Zeek off-balance. I heard him gasp as he lost his grip. The limb came smashing down on the back of my ankle with the force of a catapult. I screamed out involuntarily at the crushing pain. Zeek found a new strength that comes with panic and grabbed the log with a determination that would have allowed him to lift three logs of that size. I quickly swung my leg out of the way as Zeek broke under the strain. The limb came crashing down again with a SNAP that reverberated in the silence.

"What in the . . . ?" Old Man Zeekman announced loudly.

"Someone's here. Go find them," came a commanding voice with an odd accent.

The heavy steps again. This time at a much quicker pace.

"Hurry!" Zeek hissed as he grabbed at my coat and used my collar as leverage to thrust me upwards. Neither of us had the time to wonder about my ankle. In the darkness I couldn't see the oddly grotesque angle from which it hung at the bottom my leg.

Using Zeek as a crutch, I hopped for a few steps, sending jolts of pain up my leg. The thick brush was hard enough to get through without trying it on one leg. A rut in the path grabbed the toe of my good foot and threatened to lay me flat. Involuntarily, I stepped down on my broken ankle, trying to catch myself.

From the moment of contact, a searing pain shot up my leg and burned its way through my entire body. My scream was as unintentional as the misguided step. I found myself on my back, clenching my teeth and pounding the ground in an effort to shake the torture. Slowly the pain eased to a steady, pulsating throb. I took a slow, steady breath, hoping to appease my suffering.

As I gradually came out of my tortured haze, I could hear Zeek's worried breathing. Before I could even think the situation through, I detected the cause of his concern. Old Man Zeekman had apparently reached the back corner of the warehouse.

The thick brush served as a natural blockade which may have convinced him that the search was useless had he not heard my cry. But after only a moment's pause, we could hear him break through the first few feet, swearing the whole time.

Once I realized what was happening, I tried to lift myself up to a run, but Zeek laid a firm hand on my shoulder. Then I could tell he was feeling around in the darkness. He had a plan. He lifted something fairly heavy; it took both of his hands. With concerted effort, he heaved it towards the back of the thicket. The sound of the rock breaking through the smaller branches and twigs mimicked a person breaking through to a get-away.

It fooled Old Man Zeekman. The noise interrupted his determined march, and he stood silently for a moment. He must have decided on the cause for the disguised sounds.

"And . . . don't come back! This here's private property," he bellowed into the darkness. Then he began his routine swearing as he made his way back through the heavy brush.

We caught a glimpse of his outline when he finally reached the corner and paused before he turned to go back to the entrance of the warehouse. Through a break in the thicket, I could clearly make out a heavy, blunt object that he now drug on the ground. It looked like a club with squared off edges. I shuddered to think what he had planned to use it for.

Much to my surprise, Zeek let out a quiet sarcastic chuckle. "Can you imagine him thinking he could even swing that thing in here?" he whispered.

The image of him drawing it back, cracking it on several tree limbs and brush, and then forcefully swinging, only to be stopped by more tree trunks and wild undergrowth suddenly became funny. I could visualize the cartoon version of Old Man Zeekman, cracking the club on a huge stump, then the waves of vibration moving back up through the club to his arms and into his body.

I chuckled quietly too.

Shifting my weight slightly caused another thunderbolt of shocking pain; I became blanketed by a heavy, suffocating worry.

"What do we do now?" I asked into the darkness. So far, Zeek had come up with all of the answers, so I was more than willing to let him take control.

"We could stay here all night," he offered.

"No way," I objected. "My folks don't even know where I am. They'd kill me."

"Yea," he agreed. "And my dad would know it was me out here if I didn't come home. Then I'd really get it."

"I wish we could get some help," Zeek said, more to himself than to me.

"Wait a minute!" I dug in my pocket. "My cell." I felt for the power button and prayed for the battery to still have life. Why didn't I ever remember to charge it?

The dim light glowed eerily in the thick undergrowth. The low battery warning was on, but I was ready to punch in a number. I hesitated. What number?

"What are you waiting for?" Zeek's confused voice interrupted my thoughts.

"I'm not sure who to call."

"Your parents?" Zeek offered, as if stating the obvious.

"No, won't work. I don't want to waste what little battery I have. They won't hear their cell at the game. They'd have no reason to think . . . " I hesitated again.

"The cops?" He paused for a beat. "Yea, I think you need to call them," Now Zeek sounded more confident.

"I don't know, like 9-1-1? This isn't really an emergency."

"Really? What is it?" His question lingered in the darkness.

"Well, yea, I guess." By now the light on my cell had gone dark, so I pressed the power button again. With a new-found determination, I punched in the 3 digits and mentally began rehearsing what I would say when the dispatcher answered. I was all ready for the standard, “9 - 1- 1, what is your emergency please?”

I waited. No ring. I pulled the cell away from my ear and felt my heart drop when I couldn’t raise even a flicker of light. I tried repeatedly, pressing the power button and holding it for a ridiculous amount of time.

Dumb! Dumb! Unbelievably dumb! Why carry a cell phone but never remember to charge it? How many times have my parents gotten after me about this very thing? Useless! That’s what this cell is - totally useless without a battery. That’s what I am - useless! Oh God, I am totally useless. Please help! It was a prayer of little words, but perhaps the most desperate call for help I had ever attempted.

I didn’t say a word to Zeek. I didn’t have to. He knew. “Well, let’s get out of here,” he offered.

“Sounds easy enough, but . . .” my voice betrayed my thoughts.

“Guess there’s no point trying to cross that fence with your foot. Anyway, it doesn’t lead anywhere but out of town. We’d have to circle back around, and it’s wide open out there. We’d be seen if anyone was looking.” He paused for a moment, and then decided, “We have to go back the way we came.”

“The way we came?” I echoed in disbelief. “We can’t do that.” I tried the cell again, just in case.

“We’ll stay close to the side as we go back, then when we get near the front, we can veer off towards that line of trees that goes along the street, remember?”

I did remember them once he mentioned it; maybe his talent for planning our escape had come from practice, lots of practice. Something told me that was exactly the case, but whatever the reason, I was lucky he was there.

Just a month ago, I never would have imagined myself in this situation with Zeek. And there I was, feeling as if we were in the whole thing together, as if we had been friends for life.

Zeek stood up and held out a hand to support me as I got up. It felt like all of the blood and weight in my body rushed to my injured ankle. I inhaled sharply at the pounding, searing pain. Automatically, I lifted my knee up so I could touch my ankle, thinking maybe I could give it support or just check to see if it was swelling. When I followed the unnatural jutting angle that was now puffed full of fluid, I almost screamed with fear.

"You ok?" Zeek whispered.

"It's worse than I thought." My teeth began chattering and I zipped my jacket up to block the night air.

"Here," Zeek swung my arm around his shoulder and grabbed at my waist. "I'll help."

He was strong for his thin frame, and for a moment he reminded me of wiry Brazon. As we walked he carried a good deal of my weight, so we inched along in an odd procession.

Zeek broke the silence with a barely audible, "Hang in there. We've almost made it."

After a few more unsteady strides, I could see a break in the thicket. I sat down hard on a sturdy fallen tree, not yet ready to leave the safe cover.

"C'mon. We better keep going. It's probably half-time already."

The game. I had completely forgotten it. It was as if the moment we reached the warehouse, we stepped through a portal door into a whole new world. A dangerous, painful world. And now as we could see the door again, memories of the old world came rushing back.

With several more unsteady hops, we were standing at the unprotected corner of the warehouse. The pain was ratcheting up as my ankle hung. I wavered between not caring if we ever made it back and wanting to race home, oblivious to any danger that might follow. But as I crept around the corner, I suddenly felt like a sitting duck.

There I was, out in the open, with a twisted piece of baggage attached to the bottom of my leg. There was no place to hide here. Zeek could run and make his get-away, but I was stuck there with my crippled ankle attached to me like a lead weight.

I frantically tried my cell again, hoping that I could at least send a quick text. Nothing. Not even a hint of life. Zeek slid silently down a few inches, easing his way forward. After experimenting with several different positions, I found that by leaning the bulk of my weight back against the side of the warehouse, I could slide and hop simultaneously, though certainly not effortlessly. I followed at a distance, careful to take small breaks and not to overdo, fearing a sudden cramp or a break in my balance, either of which could cause me to fall and be discovered.

I saw the end of the warehouse approaching, and then glanced over to the group of trees that lined the street. The gap between the two was not too wide, maybe ten to fifteen yards. I wondered at the correct ways to maneuver that distance: crawling on my stomach and allowing my foot to drag? I shuddered at the thought of it even touching the ground. Maybe doing an army crawl, trying to keep my foot in the air?

My thoughts were interrupted by a sudden boom from within the warehouse. “Where are they?” an irritated voice laced with a menacing tone made us freeze in our places. In an instant I begged God for protection.

Were they still looking for us? I thought we had really fooled Old Man Zeekman. Had they heard us making our way back? No, that was impossible! I could barely hear the soft crackling of grass and leaves underfoot out in the still night.

I allowed myself to slowly look behind me to where the sound seemed to break through. Several feet above us was an open window which leaked the private conversation from within.

"They'll be here Mr. Bernado," came the uncharacteristically timid reply of Old Man Zeekman.

Who would be there? And when? It was suddenly obvious that they weren't looking for us. I looked to Zeek in hopes of finding some reassurance, but from the look of fear that twisted at his face, the last thing he was worried about was consoling me.

I don't know how long we stood there frozen in our respective spots, listening to the muted, shuffling footsteps from inside and the angry, indiscernible mutterings. I looked around wondering if we shouldn't make a break for the trees now before any more action. But had we waited too long? I could picture our decision to make our break happening just as the expected accomplices rounded the corner to the warehouse. No. We couldn't take that chance.

Not that Zeek would have agreed to it anyway. He was still frozen in his place, not daring to move, barely to breathe. Who was this guy that had Zeek so petrified? Surely he couldn't be that much worse than his dad, could he?

Bright lights broke through the webbing of the intertwined trees at the end of the street and announced an approaching car. We heard the engine rev and whine before choking off into silence. Then doors were opening and slamming shut almost simultaneously. I realized what a mistake it would have been to try to make a break for it. I quickly thanked the Lord for that decision.

Instinctively, I pressed against the side of the warehouse wall with such force that I felt I would soon make an indentation and become flush with it. In my mind, I was picturing that very thing happening as I heard the footsteps getting nearer and nearer. I didn't dare glance over to Zeek for fear that the subtle movement might catch their attention, yet I felt certain that Zeek, too, had pressed himself into the same position.

"Hurry up, we're late," the command pierced the stillness.

I could only guess at their purpose for being there that night. Drugs. Buying. Selling. Dealing. The tension in the air made me feel the answer. My gut twisted into a new knot.

Zeek and I slowly exhaled and took a needed gulp of air. He glanced over at me in a questioning look that made me wonder if I was suddenly in charge. I gently touched my awkwardly hanging toe to the grass. At the instant of contact with the unyielding ground, the snap of searing pain convinced me of its total uselessness. No, we'd have to wait until there was more time to try our escape plan.

I grabbed my cell one more time, knowing full well that it was totally dead. Before trying it again, I threw one more panicked plea to God. I tried to remember a verse that would increase my faith or give me the right words to say. All that came into my mind was "Let go and let God." Great, that wasn't even a Bible verse. However, I turned it into a prayer. *I'm going to let go, and let You take over.*

There was no lightning bolt, no voice from heaven, and when I tried my cell, there was no light; however, *I* felt different. A sudden calm settled over me. I realized that I was not in control. I was totally dependent on God, and that felt right.

"Sorry we're late sir," the barely audible voice filtered into the still night. That voice. I knew it. I recognized it from somewhere, but it was too faint and muffled to be sure.

"Just don't let it happen again." A hint of accent broke through the icy tone of the man obviously in charge. I felt Zeek beside me tense. "So are we gonna deal?" Again, his voice demanded immediate response.

"Oh yes, sir. You know I am." The voice replied.

"And you?" he must have been addressing the second person.

There was no reply.

"Whatsa problem, boy?" The evil hiss had attempted a gentler tone, but like a snake, it couldn't conceal its true intent.

"I don't know sir. I never done this kind of thing before. I just don't know if I can."

The unmistakable flavor of Brazon's voice came wafting through the crack. Then, just as assuredly, it came to me that the other voice was Ted Janson's. A feeling of overwhelming dread suddenly seized me, not like the panic I had felt in the thicket when we were so close to being caught. No. This was different. Very different.

This was an intense fear for someone else. The same kind that could be felt when watching a horror movie from a vantage point of seeing the deadly stalker move silently about the house while the main character, ignorant to the evil presence, goes about daily routines quite innocently. There is the temptation to scream to that poor unknowing victim to get out, to run, that horrible danger is present. Brazon was suddenly that main character and from my safe hiding place, I feared for him - a panicked fear that came with the knowledge of his dangerous position and of his ignorance.

"There's nothing to it." The impatient words of the man in charge were coated with an unnatural sweetness.

"You said you needed the money, didn't ya?" prompted Ted.

"Well, yea, but . . . "

"But nothing. This is the easiest way to get your hands on some real cash. So c'mon, what are you waiting for?"

There was an unsettled silence, and I could tell they were waiting for Brazon's decision. From off in the distance, a whine sounded. It grew in volume and intensity as it seemed to get nearer.

"Who called the cops?" the accent was heavy and the tone icy.

There must have been a lot of shaking heads and silent looks, for not a word was spoken. Heavy footsteps raced to the front and the sliding door heaved open on its track. Then everything seemed to happen at once.

We could hear the first engine rev to life as the car doors opened and slammed shut on the second car. Eerie red and blue flashing lights broke through the darkness and flooded the scene. Time seemed to stand still.

"Who called 9-1-1?" The first police officer demanded as he got out of his car.

There was an awkward silence.

"That would be us," Zeek answered as he stepped out of the darkness and moved to the front of the building.

Chapter 10

"The 9-1-1 call?" I tried to gather my thoughts. "But my cell was dead - I didn't think the call went through." There was too much going on. The back of the ambulance was so bright, and metallic, and sterile. My voice seemed to echo in the portable emergency room. I tried again to focus as I noticed the officer's intense look. I rubbed my eyes and pinched the bridge of my nose in an effort to gather my thoughts. If only they had waited to give me the pain killer, I was sure I could have done a better job answering his questions.

From the time the sirens pierced through the night air and the bright red lights assaulted the scene, I had kept my wits about me. Even when the gurney clicked into place and the paramedics carefully stabilized my leg and lifted me onto the rolling bed, I answered their questions with unnatural calm.

"No, I can't feel my toes. Yes, I know my name and what day it is. No, my parents haven't been called. Yes, I know their cell number. No, I'm not allergic to any medications. Yes, I know it will be ok."

But now I was losing focus. The 9-1-1 call. Was that what the police officer was asking about? "Yes, I made the call. But how did it go through? My cell died. I - I didn't get to talk to anyone."

Through my haze, the officer explained something about all 9-1-1 calls being traced to their origin and police officers being sent to the location. He went on about the practice ensuring that help would come even if someone were incapacitated and unable to give even the most basic information. I smiled and nodded, thinking that he would believe that explanation, but I knew better. The same peace that settled over me during our ordeal assured me that God was the One who had orchestrated everything from beginning to end.

I closed my eyes. I had a feeling that the policeman wanted more answers, but my eyelids were too heavy to keep open. He would have to wait.

When I woke up, I was in a hospital room. It was oddly quiet, with steady beeping and clicking from machines that were somewhere close behind me. I tried to lift my head and look around, but it felt like someone had filled me full of lead. I blinked a few more times and closed my eyes again.

I must have slept through the night because the next time I opened my eyes, bright sunlight was pushing through the cracks of the window, brightening the room. I glanced around through slitted eyes, trying to get my bearings.

"Hey - he's awake!" My mom's relieved voice broke the silence.

"Hi," I managed.

A nurse hurried in and routinely took my pulse, temperature, and blood pressure. I tried to coherently answer her questions, but felt like I was in a fog. I must have satisfied her because she hustled off promising to ask about pain relief.

"Where am I?"

"They moved you to a regular room after your surgery."

"Surgery?"

"Yes," she answered as she brushed my hair back from my forehead. "You have been out for quite awhile. They had to set your ankle and put a pin in it. You had a nasty break."

"Uh-huh." I knew that much. I still felt like I was two steps behind everyone, groggy and unable to catch up.

"Do you remember what happened?" My dad was on my other side. I rolled my head in his direction.

"I think so."

"I bet you have a lot of questions. I know we do."

I thought that his comment should worry me, but the way he said it left me feeling that he wasn't too mad. I wasn't able to stay awake long enough to worry about it. I let my head roll back to a natural position and closed my eyes.

Sleep seemed to dictate the schedule for the rest of the day. I would wake up long enough to be poked and prodded by the nurses, given more pain meds, ask my parents a couple of questions, then slip back off to sleep. I had hazy dreams about a police officer at the warehouse helping me to sit down and covering me with his coat. I could hear the static of the radio as he called for an ambulance. I had a picture in my mind of four people lined up with their hands spread out on a vehicle and their legs straddled wide as police officers handcuffed them.

The last time I woke, it was to the voice of a policeman talking with my parents. He had a notebook in his hand and looked ready for an interrogation. When he noticed me, he smiled.

"Well, you've had quite a time, haven't you?"

I nodded.

"Feel like answering some questions?"

I nodded again.

He asked me to replay the evening from the time I saw Brazon at the football game. I did my best to recount the events with as much detail as possible. I emphasized several times how I overheard Brazon saying that he had never done anything like this before. I added that we had been friends for a long time and I didn't think he'd go through with selling drugs; he was just at the wrong place at the wrong time. He didn't say much, just wrote notes and asked a question or two. Then he explained again how my 9-1-1 call had located us, but added with a grin that the timing was rather "miraculous" in his opinion.

When I asked about Brazon, he reluctantly replied that he couldn't say much about my "friend" because it was an ongoing case.

He stood and thanked me for my part in busting a known drug dealer and promised to keep me informed as much as he could. As he left the room, Zeek poked his head in and waved his goofy wave.

"Can I come in?" he asked.

"Sure," I winced just a bit as I pushed to an upright position.

"How are you?" He looked at me hopefully.

"All good," I lied.

"Did you hear?" He looked like a kid waiting for me to open a birthday gift he brought.

"Hear what?"

"I'm staying at your house while everything gets straightened out. Your mom said she would call my mom and explain everything. I think it's going to be ok." He looked down at me with what may have been the first genuine look of happiness I had seen.

"That's really awesome!"

"While you were sleeping, your youth pastor came by. He told me that he thought God had a plan for me and that He was protecting us the whole time we were at the warehouse. What do you think?"

I paused as I looked at this unlikely friend. I realized that I couldn't wait to tell him what I thought.

Made in the USA
Middletown, DE
01 September 2017